RADIO DAYS

BY

CYNDY MUSCATEL

This book was published with the assistance of Self-Publishing Relief, a division of Writer's Relief.

© Cyndy Muscatel, 2019

Some stories included in this volume first appeared in the following publications:

"A Moment in Time," *The Penmen Review*, July 2014
"African Song," *descant*, 2002
"Anniversary Waltz," *The Legendary*, July 2011
"At the Sound of the Beep," *Jet Fuel Review*, Fall 2013
"Clueless in California," *OxMag*, Summer 2015
"Confessions of the Hot Flash Queen," *Quercus Review*, 2008
"Her Father's Daughter," *EDGE*, 2011
"Just Once," *Tower Journal*, 2014 (published as "Guilt by Association")
"Khrushchev in My Dreams," *Existere*, 2013
"Mid-Solstice Night Dreaming," *riverSedge*, 2003
"Of Pinafores and Satin Bows," *Literary Orphans*, October 2017
"One Moment in Time," *The MacGuffin*, 2012
"The Pail of Water," *13th Moon*, 2005
"Primal Fear," *Good Works Review*, 2017
"Rush to Judgment," *Main Street Rag*, Summer 2014
"Waking Up at Midnight," *Haight Ashbury*, 2007

CONTENTS

A Moment in Time

Olivia couldn't stay in bed. The silent coldness from the warm body next to her drove her out. It was past midnight as she crept down the stairs.

The wind lashed against the French doors in her living room, whistling through the cracks. The sound was her companion. She sat in the dark, sipping hot chocolate. It was nothing new, her insomnia. The only variant in the ritual was the choice of beverage. Until recently it had been scotch.

A psychic healer once told her she fought sleep, that she considered it a waste of time. Olivia had been impressed the man knew she didn't sleep well. But he was wrong. She liked to sleep and to dream. Unless her dreams were nightmares of helicopters breaking up and spilling its GI Joe-like figures helter-skelter through the air.

She shook her head, trying to erase last night's dream. She pictured the healer instead. He'd been a little older than she was. Strands of gray threaded the Chinese-straight hair falling to the middle of his back.

"How'd you know?" she'd asked him. "I've never been a good sleeper, even when I was a kid. It's because there's so much I like to do. I can't fit it all in during a day."

"That is why you push the envelope of time for bed. Your mind, it does not still, not ready to retire," he said.

Olivia figured it was an inherited trait. Her aunt had trouble sleeping, too. Aunt Rose used to say that when her head hit the pillow, all her worries came to the surface. LochNess monsters lurked. Let loose by the quiet of the night, they haunted her. Did it still happen now that she had Alzheimer's? Rose's memory length was in five-minute segments. Did Rocky, buried at three, still come to visit when the lights went out? Or did she sleep through the night, her dead son finally forgotten?

"There is so much sadness in this world." This refrain punctuated Olivia's father's last years. She'd believed it was old age, but came to realize that melancholy was his natural state. He'd just expressed it through Chopin before the stroke made his hands incapable of hitting the keys. She had loved her dad with single-minded devotion. As a child, she'd sat puppy-like at his feet.

Olivia put down the cup and buried herself into the wings of the chair. Sadness, inherited and accumulated, seeped into her bones. I am as chained by my childhood as I've ever been, she thought. The sins of the fathers, of the mothers, revisit generation after generation, Hallelujah.

Her troubles beat a tattoo in her head as loud as the rain on the roof. She used to think she could change the world—a youth's delusions. People didn't change, and neither did the world. Years before when the Berlin Wall had fallen, she'd believed people would beat their spears into pruning hooks, and there would be peace among the nations. But it was the reverse. Ancient blood feuds and greed had created a world filled with butchery and ruin. Who needed to worry about global warming when nuclear winter seemed a foregone conclusion?

She'd seen a guy this afternoon in the pet store. He'd seemed a little odd in his movements. And he scowled at everyone, except for the son by his side. Him, he just ignored. Behind them in the checkout line, she saw that scars ran down the middle of the man's head like the seam on a football.

The boy had turned to her. "I'd like a goldfish," he said. "Do you think those tanks are real expensive?"

Before Olivia could answer, the father grabbed him by the sleeve. "Esteban, shut up about the fish." His voice was like twisted metal.

In the parking lot, she'd seen them drive away. On the back of the truck, a red, white, and blue sticker proclaimed *Support Your Troops*. The pieces of their puzzle clicked into place. Olivia wondered what the man had been like before he'd been a soldier. Had he been a better father?

She'd once thought she could change the patterns of *her* family. How stupid. She hadn't done a better job than her mother—maybe worse. She'd tried—tried damn hard—she had to give herself that. Unlike her mother, Olivia hadn't pursued the career she'd wanted. It would have taken too much time away from Max and Lindsay.

The joke was on her. Her kids were still screwed up. Maybe if Max hadn't been so sick with asthma, things would have been better. Had she given so much of herself to Max that he felt stifled and Lindsay felt shortchanged?

Olivia shivered in the dark. She was no nearer sleep than she had been hours ago. She longed for whiskey. It would make her forget for a while. She started to get up, then sat back down. No, she would NOT go that route again. She'd promised herself.

She swallowed hard and settled back into the chair. "Do not dwell on the past," she said aloud. To do so would lead her into a quagmire of what-might-have-beens. She'd gone wrong somewhere with her children—you couldn't dispute the evidence. But she had to go forward. Was it the lecture on Maslow's Hierarchy of Needs in her child psychology class that had stirred up old recriminations?

"Being seen, being heard—these are the most basic of our needs after shelter and safety," her professor said. "This isn't happening for many of our kids. And I'm not talking just at the poverty level—it's at every level."

He'd peered over the top of his glasses at the class. "Parents don't even look at their kids when they talk to them. They're too busy working or driving from one activity to another. And parents don't take their eyes off the screen—whether it's television, cell phone or computer —to look into the eyes of their child, to acknowledge their existence. Without this, there's no way a child will develop self-esteem."

Olivia had cringed at the words. The professor was describing her—the way she'd been with Max and Lindsay. Always doing two things at once. She should have stopped doing so damn much for them and simply paid them more attention. Then she might have noticed the sweet pungency of the marijuana that scented Max's clothes. She might have realized that Lindsay's hours on the Internet had nothing to do with researching her paper on the Salem Witch Trials.

Robert blamed her for both of the kids' problems, but especially Lindsay's.

"You're her parent just as much as I am," she'd said in her defense.

"You're the one who was supposed to be there. How could you not know where she was going after school? Where the hell were you?"

Olivia's stomach clenched as she remembered the nightmare of filing a missing person's report, and dealing with the police. It was as if it happened yesterday instead of five years ago. They'd found Lindsay soon after, but it hadn't been soon enough. She'd never been the same. Neither had Olivia or Robert. Or their relationship. Robert barely talked to her. The loneliness drove her first to drink, then back to college to get her counseling degree. If she couldn't help her own children, she would learn to help others. And she could fill up her hours with work.

"Most babies are looked at. In fact, the mother makes eye-to-eye contact all the time, bringing her face close to her infant's," the professor said that morning. "A baby is accepted for what he or she is. If they're not, they wither physically and emotionally. Or they become sociopaths. When does it start? When does a child begin to feel unimportant?"

He took off his glasses, setting them on the lectern. "When did it happen to you?"

He'd dismissed class a few minutes later, after giving them the assignment to write about the last time they'd felt seen by their parents. Most of the students in the class were in their twenties—they wouldn't have to delve as far back. For Olivia, it would be an ancient history assignment.

She sighed and turned on the lamp next to her chair. She couldn't stop thinking about Max, about Lindsay. She took her cup to the kitchen, rinsed it, and put it in the dishwasher. She thought she might be too old to do this assignment but she'd give it a try.

A few minutes later, she sat in front of her computer, eyes closed, trying to remember the last time she'd felt seen by her parents. Her mother, probably never. It was rare for a bi-polar narcissist to think of someone other than herself. Olivia's childhood had revolved around her mother's moods. Her dad had acted as a buffer. She remembered, too, his patience and care. He'd sat on her bed and patted her back when she couldn't sleep because she was afraid of death. He talked her, soothed her until finally she grew out of the terrors.

Olivia's fingers flew over the keyboard. She'd forgotten this time in her childhood but remembering created a torent of memories. She re-read what she had written, then leaned back in the desk chair. She was finished.

A tear rolled down her cheek. She wiped it away. Could the last time she'd felt seen by a parent been when she was so small? Maybe she was just being melodramatic. Her parents had come to her performances, to her concerts, to her graduation. They'd seen her then, hadn't they? Or was it just her accomplishments reflecting themselves?

In the bathroom off her office, Olivia looked at herself in the mirror. She stared into her eyes, trying to see the person behind them. She reached out a hand to touch her reflected face, but found it impossible. She couldn't penetrate the hard coldness of the glass.

From the bedroom down the hall, she heard the clock radio turn on. Though she hadn't really slept, it was time to get up. She wasn't sure how she'd make it through the day.

A F R I C A N S O N G

The first time Ashley awoke it was to the sound of drums and a throbbing in her head. A song played through it all, one of harmony and safety.

Her eyelids flickered as she tried to open them. A man's voice close to her ear, said, "She wakes."

A rustling of material was followed by a cool hand on her forehead. Fingers moved towards the nucleus of throbbing in her temple. She tensed against the coming agony. But instead the shooting pain lessened, and a melody of relief flooded her. She slept again.

When Ashley next opened her eyes, all was quiet except for the peaceful hymn singing through her. It was dark, as if a veil hung before her face. She leaned on her elbow, trying to lift herself into a sitting position. She only succeeded in raising the drummers in her right temple. She lay back, exhausted.

As her eyes became used to the blackness, she could make out shapes near her. She heard a sigh. She realized that the form so close was another person. Trying to keep the drummers still, she turned and saw that others slept nearby.

She hadn't been in Africa long, but she reckoned this was the women's sleeping quarters of some tribe. Why she knew this, she wasn't certain. Why she felt safe and protected, she didn't even question.

Her hand floated in front of her face, its pale whiteness visible. She lowered it to the soft woven fiber of the mat beneath her, then inched her fingers beyond its border. If she had been found by a migrant tribe, she would be sleeping on open ground. The hardness of the dirt floor signified a village.

How long had she been here? And what had happened? Memories collected to be sifted through. She'd been on safari with Helen and Jake, but that was weird. Why would she be with them? Even though they worked in the same accounting office, she wasn't that close to either. Then she remembered Helen had told her about the ad she'd heard on the radio.

"You can go on safari in Kenya and Tanzania. They have a really good deal for the month of February," Helen had said.

"Are you going to do it?" Ashley asked.

"Yep, and Jake, too."

"Maybe I'll go to," Ashley said.

"I'm going to Africa to find myself," she'd told her mother before she left Boston. Ever since 9/11, she'd felt lost.

"That sounds like a damn cliché," her mother said. "I think it's a terrible idea. You're just now getting on your feet."

Ashley had left New York after the planes hit the two towers. She'd come home to Boston, barely able to function. Months later, she was able to work, at least. Ashley knew her mother was afraid to shift the balance. She went anyway.

An image of sitting in a jeep flitted into Ashley's mind.. She could see jungle plants on the side of the road. Still coated in raindrops from the cloudburst that had passed on, they steamed in the hot sun like spinach in a glass pot. Jake and Helen sat in front of her. The guide pointed out the herd of water buffalo to the right. She remembered picking up her new digital camera. . . .

Clashing cymbals of pain pounded across her forehead. She winced and gave up trying to piece the memories into a coherent whole.

After a while, the pain receded and she could think again. Slowly, she began an inventory of her body. When she touched her temple, she felt something wet and bulky there. She brought her fingers to her nose, smelling the tang of herbs that must have been mixed with mud to create a poultice. Continuing to explore her face, she felt a stickiness and welts crisscrossing her cheeks. She drew her hand away with a shudder.

"Are you all right?" The voice was sweet, melodious, healing.

Ashley looked up, but the darkness revealed little of the person who spoke. She returned her hand to her face and retraced the welt marks.

The woman in the shadows seemed to understand. "You must have fallen. We found you twisted in the vines, your face so marked, your head bloody. But we will talk more at the sun's rising. You must sleep now, so you can heal. Drink some of this." She leaned over Ashley, helping her sit, holding out a cup.

Ashley knew without any doubt she could trust the woman. She drank freely of the milky substance. She lay back. As the woman changed the herb and mud dressing on her head, she listened to the soft song the woman sang. It was a lullaby of sunshine and rainbows and gentle breezes.

"You are home, now," the woman crooned. "You have come back to your heart."

"I have been lost, now I am found," Ashley said.

The woman nodded. Her turban caught threads of moonlight seeping through the holes in the ragged sides of the tent and glinted golden in Ashley's eyes. Now lit as if by fire, Ashley could see the ebony of the woman's features.

"You look like Ashwanti," she said.

"That is my name."

"But that can't be. Ashwanti is a carved mask my father brought back from Tanzania before I was born. It's on the wall in the den."

The woman's lips tightened, but she didn't speak.

Violins screeched a warning in Ashley's head. Her heart beat fast in time to their rhythm. She moved restlessly on the pallet. "How can your name be the same as a mask's?" she asked.

"To some things, there are no answers," the woman said.

Ashley looked at Ashwanti, at how her face seemed to be melting. She felt sweat trickle down her own forehead. "It is so hot. In Boston, it was snowing."

"You will never need worry about cold again."

"Really? Why?"

"You have come home to your heart."

"Oh, yes." Ashley smiled and sighed back into the smoothness of the braided reeds. "I was lost, now I am found," she sang.

The woman's gentle fingers pressed Ashley's eyelids closed. "Sleep, now."

"Yes, yes. I will."

Ashley turned on her side, the song of homecoming soothing her. She realized just before sleep overtook her that Ashwanti had spoken to her in Swahili and she understood every word.

ANNIVERSARY WALTZ

An air-conditioned breeze blew through the ship's dining salon, disturbing the fronds on the palm trees near the waterfall feature. It also disturbed the few strands of hair Adam had combed over his scalp an hour before. He patted at his head trying to salvage the damage. Every time he took his hand away, wisps of hair flew up like strings tied to helium balloons.

"Oh, what the hell," he muttered. "Who cares anyway?"

He'd wanted to shave his head and be done with it, but Lindy wouldn't hear of it. She had him taking Propecia and using Rogaine. One of those was playing havoc with what was left of his libido so he was done with them too. He'd go to the barber tomorrow and look like Mr. Clean by dinnertime.

He finished his Glen Fiddich and signaled for another.

"Adam, you're drinking too much."

Adam crunched on a piece of ice, grinding it under his molars as if he were a wood chip shredder. It took a moment to loosen his jaws before he could answer his wife. "Lindy, that's not exactly a news flash. I always drink too much."

That stopped her, Adam thought, chuckling on the inside. On the outside he grabbed the drink the waiter set in front of him and took a healthy swig.

"You shouldn't say things like that," Lindy said.

Adam rolled his eyes at her hurt tone. It was as shallow as the fake pool and waterfall in the corner. The words in his head prompted him to look at the waterfall. Damn, he'd told himself he wouldn't—every time he did, his blood pressure went to infinity and beyond. The waterfall was so fucking stupid it pissed him off. Why would anyone design a ship's dining room with a water feature? Wasn't there already enough water in the ocean outside? What—they needed more inside, for Christ's sake?

"I said that you shouldn't say things like that!"

It had been a long time since he'd been grateful to hear his wife's voice. Now it broke the waterfall's spell. He tore his gaze away from it and eyed her.

"Why not?"

"It doesn't sound right."

"It's true, though. Don't you always say that telling the truth is important?"

"Oh, Adam, you're being impossible. I promised myself I would ignore you when you're like this." She looked away from him, then took out a lipstick and retouched her lips.

He knew she'd had her make up done that afternoon because he'd already seen the bill on the ship's channel 44 running account. Why the hell did she have to fuss? They were on this miserable cruise, just the two of them. Who did she have to impress?

But there was something so…he groped for a word that would describe it. Defenseless? Vulnerable? Sad? Something anyway that made him feel bad as she covered lips already painted to perfection.

He sighed. He could be an asshole. He knew it. One of his grandkids was scared to death of him. Told his mother that Gramps growled like a grizzly. At first Adam had been pissed at the kid. "Be a man," he wanted to say to him. Had almost said. Then he'd thought of his own grandfather. He remembered that sneering old man sitting by the Philco radio in his apartment. The perpetual scowl on Grandpa's face would have scared the shit out of any kid, not just Adam.

"Go up and give Grandpa a kiss," his father had told him. Adam hadn't wanted to go near the smelly old man. He turned his face into his mother's skirts.

"Don't be a sissy, for Christ's sake." His father grabbed him hard by the shoulder. "Didn't I just show you the razor strops in Grandpa's bathroom that he used to hit me with? You want a taste of that? That'll make you into a man sooner than later."

Adam shut down the memory as soon as he could. He'd kept it buried, too, until he saw the fear on his own grandson's face. He never wanted to think of himself as weak, but tried to be less gruff with his grandkids since then. He liked the little buggers. Even when they climbed all over him, he liked them.

Not that he saw them much anymore. Since Diana died, he'd grown apart from his kids. Especially since he'd married Lindy, they almost never came to visit. His two sons were so busy driving their kids to practices and classes they barely had time to work an eight-hour day. He shook his head in disgust. Adam, Jr. and Rob had wives that demanded they do an equal share at home. What horse shit!

Diana had never pulled that kind of crap on him. Okay, so she forced him to do Indian Guides with the boys, but that had been it. For Christ's sake, he'd been traveling so much when the boys were young, he had no time for their activities. Creating his business took all of his concentration. He'd had zero time to waste. So maybe he wasn't close to his kids, but look what he'd built for them.

"Why are you frowning?" Lindy asked.

He glared at her. "I'm not frowning."

"Okay." She closed her purse with a snap." Whatever you say."

Oh, crap, here we go, he thought. He'd better apologize to keep the peace. It wasn't her fault that she drove him crazy. He'd made his bed and now he was wallowing in it.

"Lindy." Adam cleared his throat. "Sorry. I just get edgy not having anything to do."

Her attitude adjusted in a nanosecond. Without even taking a sip of her wine, Adam marveled.

She gave him the brilliant smile he'd paid through the nose for. "It's okay. I forgive you."

Under the table, he clenched his fist. Just one sentence and he was ready to kill her again. Next, she'll bat her eyelashes at me, he thought.

Isn't that how she got his attention in the first place? He'd been in a bad mood when he'd boarded the plane five years ago. He'd been on his way to Paris for business two months after Diana died. Lindy had been his flight attendant in first class. When she asked if he wanted another whiskey, he'd snapped, "Hell, no!" She'd looked so frightened, he felt like a jerk, and was a model passenger for the remainder of the flight. Somehow she'd spent her layover in Paris laying him in his hotel room at the Meurice.

The vacuous smiles had worked then—he'd thought she was just an upbeat person. God knew, he needed something positive in his life after watching Diana go through cancer hell. But that was then.

Now, he knew there was nothing easy about the woman at his table. Though she looked harmless, she was Machiavellian in getting her way. Meanwhile, each empty smile made him want to bash his head into a wall.

"There's no fool like an old fool," Diana's sister Carin had taunted on his wedding day to Lindy.

He'd figured Carin was just jealous on Diana's account. "Tsk, tsk," he'd said to get her goat. "You, the English teacher, using a cliché?"

She gave him the Diana look—the one that saw right through you. "Somehow the occasion begs for it," she said.

He'd told her to go to hell, and hadn't seen her since. But every once in a while, a refrain snorted in his head like a Greek Chorus that had slipped its traces: *You are a fucking cliché, Adam. A fucking cliché.*

"Isn't it just so chichi," Lindy breathed, indicating the ship's dining room and the sequined passengers flashing in the candlelight.

"She-she? Oh, yes...so chichi." Adam couldn't keep the sarcasm out of his voice. He wondered if Lindy noticed. Diana would have. But he'd never have been on this ship with Diana. She hated this kind of pretension as much as he did.

He thought of his wife, not as she'd been when the cancer had whittled her down, but as she was in her prime. A big woman with a big laugh and a take-no-prisoners attitude, she'd never taken an ounce of shit from him. He'd believed she could beat anything. He was so shocked when she died...when she just stopped breathing.

He took a gulp of the Scotch.

"I knew you'd like this cruise," Lindy was saying. "Aren't you glad, darling, we took this trip, just the two of us, alone, together. None of your kids, or business partners or your ol' golf buddies?"

Adam would have given his first million for any of the above mentioned. He slipped a finger into his collar. Damn thing was so tight he couldn't breathe. And it was so hot. Christ, why did they make you wear a tux in the Caribbean?

Before he could incriminate himself and tell Lindy what he really thought, the waiter appeared at his elbow. "Mr. Butler, here's your entrée."

The thick T-bone looked perfectly cooked—charred on the outside, but running with juices. The fries looked crisp and the spinach, creamy. One good thing on the ship—the food was outstanding.

Lindy wrinkled her noise. "That food looks disgusting."

"What are you talking about? It looks fantastic." Adam picked up his knife and fork.

"Steak is so high in cholesterol. Think of all the fat. And the same goes for the fries. The spinach isn't even healthy."

The best part of his day and she was going to ruin it for him? "Lindy, for Christ's sake, eat your own meal and leave me alone. I'm old enough to know what I want to eat."

"But, Adam, it isn't healthy. Your heart, your blood pressure...."

Speaking of blood pressure, Adam felt his spike. "Just butt out, okay. Is that clear enough?"

"Don't shout—people are looking. You're embarrassing me," she said.

"Well, you're smothering me. My mother has been dead for twenty-five years. I don't need another one."

Lindy's mouth thinned, displacing some of the lipstick. "Fine. I won't look after your welfare anymore."

"Bingo! You finally figured it out. Now let's eat."

Lindy made an angry sound and stood up. "Like I said before, you are impossible."

"Sit down and eat."

"I'm going to the Ladies Room."

"Your food will get cold."

"I am having Salad Nicoise," she said.

Adam watched her stalk towards the door. He shrugged. As he turned back to his food, he caught the people at the next table staring at him.

"Enjoy the show?" he asked.

Like synchronized swimmers, the six of them swiveled their heads away.

Adam grinned. He couldn't care less what other people thought.

He rubbed his hands. "Alone at last. Now I can enjoy every mouthful," he said aloud.

He cut into his steak. *Ah, perfectly cooked.* He crammed a large piece into his mouth. He chewed, enjoying the succulent, if slightly tough meat. He swallowed it down with a gulp of scotch.

He wasn't worried about Lindy. He knew she'd come back after she'd cooled down. She wouldn't want to miss a photo op—it was their anniversary, and she loved memorializing each one. He ate a few fries, licking his fingers, then cut another piece of steak.

Now this is living, he thought. He sank his teeth into the beef. Barely chewing, he swallowed the whole mouthful. It caught in his throat.

He coughed, trying to dislodge the meat. Nothing happened.

He coughed again. Nada. Beads of sweat formed on his receded hairline. Making loud gagging noises, he put his hand to his throat. He felt like he was in a chokehold. *That damned collar was so tight!*

The people at the next table glanced towards him, then away as if he were a Silverback gorilla ready to charge. Still choking, he lurched up from the table. He wasn't going to make a damn fool of himself in front of everyone.

He'd almost made it to the door when he realized he couldn't breathe at all. As he began to black out, he tripped on a hose sticking out of the waterfall. His last thought as he toppled face first into the water was, *this fucking pool.*

"It was the waterfall that saved you," Lindy, sounding chipper, told him the next morning.

Adam looked at her through his one good eye. The other was swollen shut, already black and blue from his fall. His head was wrapped in bandages. He ached from his head to his feet.

"How the hell did the waterfall save me?" he asked. "I fell into the fucking thing."

"Well, the ship's doctor saw you trip on the hose. And he noticed that you were grabbing at your throat." She put her hand to her own throat and rubbed.

Adam's eye squinted as he tried to see her better. Her bright smile and lipstick were gone. Her cheeks trailed tear lines of mascara.

"So, when someone started to help you up, he rushed over and did the Heimlich on you, no questions asked." She swallowed like it was a hard thing to do. "Thank God he did. People told me your face was blue."

Tears filled her eyes as she took his hand and held it tight.

Adam shook his head. Lindy looked genuinely distressed, like she actually cared about him. *Jesus!* And the damn waterfall he hated saved his life? That was a Ripley's. Things he'd been certain about seemed not certain at all.

He shook his head, then regretted it. The throbbing returned full throttle. He closed his eyes. He was tired now. Maybe he could make sense out of everything later.

Just before he fell asleep, he smiled. They'd had to shave his head to take care of his injuries. Hot damn! Talk about things going your way.

He wondered what his chances were of getting a bacon cheeseburger for lunch.

At The Sound Of The Beep

Hi, you've reached Ana and Jeff Winston. We can't take your call right now, but please leave your message at the sound of the beep, and we'll get right back to you.

April 1, 4:00 p.m.

Jeff, I know what you've been doing. You've been helping yourself to my trust. And that isn't too smart. That is against the *law*. You can't just take my money. I'm going to call the IRS on you. How do you think you'll like prison? You won't have all your fancy friends, will you? They'll desert you like the dog you are.

April 1, 4:30 p.m.

You can't just steal people's money and get away with it. You fucking asshole, you thought you were pretty smart getting control of my trust. That's what a big brother is for, right? To watch over you. Like you'd ever help me. All you want is my money.

April 1, 5:00 p.m.

You thought you could do whatever you wanted, didn't you, Jeff? Just take poor Johnny's money. So what if Johnny doesn't have the cash to buy gas or food. What do you care, you in your fancy house in California?

April 1, 11:30 p.m.

Jeff, just because you told me to stop calling you doesn't mean that I will. I'm not afraid of you, big shot. I'll call you any fuckin' time I want. I don't care if it's upsetting Ana. Tough shit. You give me back my money so I can go out—then I won't call you.

April 2, 10:00 a.m.
Hi, Ana. This is Robert from Guardianship, Inc. returning your call. I haven't talked to you since you moved to California. Well, anyway, you guessed it. John is off his meds. He needs to be hospitalized, but, as you know, we can't commit him unless he proves a danger to himself or someone else. I know how annoying John's calls can be. Try to get your phone company to block them. Here's another piece of advice. Never answer his calls. Never return his calls. He lives for that. Once he gets started, he doesn't stop. Believe me, I know. We had to change our number at the office and at home.

April 2, 11:00 a.m.
Mr. Winston? This is Calabasas Cardiology. We need you to come in and redo part of your nuclear stress test. It's nothing to concern yourself over. The results in one section were unclear. Call Rhonda to make an appointment.

April 2, 3:00 p.m.
Hello, Jeffrey, it's me, Johnny. I'm not going away. You've got a big problem—*me*. And there's only one way to get rid of me, Jeff. Kill me. Yeah, why don't you kill me? You know some guys who could do it. Just call one of them and say, 'I have this problem with my brother.' Yeah, put out a contract on me. Have one of your goons murder me.

April 2, 5:30 p.m.
This is Verizon returning your call, Mr. Winston. Unfortunately, in the state of California, you cannot block one person from calling your number. We have a service, call intercept, but it will intercept every call made to you. If you would like to add this service to your account, call us back.

April 3, 2:00 a.m.
Hello there, Jeffrey. This is Frank—Frank Sinatra. I heard on the radio that you're singing at the Copa with my friend, Sammy. Hey, Jeff, you used to buy my records and I liked you. But if you keep up this singing, I'm going to cut off your fucking balls.

April 3, 2:13 a.m.

Sammy is dead, Jeff, and so is Dean. Look in the fucking mirror. You aren't Frank. You can't sing worth shit. You ain't no Sammy Davis either. If I ever catch you trying to play in *Oceans Thirteen*, I *will* cut your nuts off.

April 3, Noon

Hi, Jeff. This is Robert from Guardianship returning your call. I also left a message on your cell. I just wanted to let you know that our hands are pretty tied up here. We can't even get into John's house right now. He's changed all the locks on his doors and won't answer when we call him. Schizophrenia is a weird deal. And John's never easy, even when he does take his meds.

April 3, 2:00 p.m.

Hi, Ana. It sounds like Jeff's brother is really bad this time. Those phone calls day and night can't be easy to take. You're sure that something can't be done to hospitalize John? God, I remember what a great kid he was. What was he, thirteen, when you got married? He was such a sweetheart. Life can be such shit. Oh well. What can we do? Call your brother.

April 3, 5:00 p.m.

Jeff. Jeff, are you there? Answer the fucking phone. You think you can just ignore me?

April 3, 6:00 p.m.

Hello, Jeff. I got your message. I don't know what you're complaining about. You moved away from Portland so you wouldn't have to deal with any problems—with Mom or with our brother. You left it all to me to deal with. I have such a bad cold, but Mom calls me at eight o'clock this morning, saying her hand is heavy. I have to get out of bed and take her to the emergency room.

If you don't think Robert and the Guardianship are doing a good job, quit complaining, come on up to Portland, and hire somebody new.

April 3, 6:20 p.m.

Jeff, I know what you're trying to do. You're trying to block my calls. I'm really bugging you, aren't I, big man? I think you have a problem— John's the problem. What are you going to do about it? I ain't quitting. I'm havin' way too much fun. I guess you may want to have me assassinated, huh? I better stay away from windows.

April 3, 8:00 p.m.

Jeff, goddamn it. You blocked ten of my calls. I couldn't even get to your answering machine. But now I'm back on track, and I have all the time in the world. Here's the deal, asshole. I'm not stopping. Your only choice is to attack John. Have me murdered. Step up and beat the Lord, tough guy. Have me killed. Call your man, Mr. Sinatra, and have me shot.

April 4, 9:00 a.m.

Hi, Ana, it's your brother. You make me laugh. I can just see you picking up the phone and putting it down as fast as you can. How many times did you say Johnny called in ten minutes? Eight? At least he finally stopped.

April 4, 1:30 p.m.

Mom, it's Kim. I'm just having an awful day. Everything is going wrong... Sorry for crying, but I can't help it. I hate going to work. I hate it.

April 4, 3:00 p.m.

Thanks for the call back, Mom, but I'm tired of just sucking it up all the time. My boss is just a jerk. He came in with a hangover this morning and started yelling at everyone about how we weren't doing our work. I can't take it anymore—I'm going to start looking for another job.

April 4, 8:00 p.m.

I am very aware, Mother, that I'm a single mother. Maybe you and Dad think I can't afford to quit my job, but I can't afford to be this stressed. You just don't understand how bad it is. Ever since I moved back to Portland, I've been trying to make enough money for me and Leo to live comfortably. I don't want to ask you for money either. But it's a lot of pressure.

April 4, 11:10 p.m.

I know you think you married Kim Novak, Jeff, like you're one of the Rat Pack. You think you're just like Frank, with beautiful women around. But Ana ain't no Kim Novak. She looks like shit.

April 5, 1:30 a.m.

I hate you so much. I wish you were dead. As a matter of fact, I'm going to say a prayer for your death. Yeah, right now. *Dear God, Listen to my prayer. My brother has already had two heart attacks. One of them almost killed him. His heart is weak. Do the job, Almighty God—give him another heart attack. He doesn't deserve to live. Get him off the face of the earth. Do this for me, your faithful servant, John, and I will always be in your gratitude, O Lord.*

April 5, 10:00 a.m.

This is Calabasas Cardiology again. Dr. Martin wants you to redo the nuclear stress test as soon as possible. Again, don't be overly concerned. He just wants to make sure that the results are clearer. Call the office today.

April 5, 2:30 p.m.

Hi, Ana. It's Betty. Sorry I missed your call. Yes, Derrick would do the phone harassment too. I don't think he ever used real foul language, but he'd go off his meds and the obsessions would start in…and the voices. Once he threw away a radio because he said the voices would come through on the FM. It's real typical that your brother-in-law calls late at night. Derrick would sleep most of the day and stay up all night. Look, I want you to call me back so we can talk in person, but until we can connect, go online to N-A-M-I. That's the National Alliance on Mental Illness. There's some good information. Take care and call. I don't know what I'd have done without a support system.

April 5, 8:00 p.m.

You better start answering my calls, Jeff, or I'm going to hurt you real bad. You think you can just ignore me, but I know how to get to you. Just you watch, asshole.

April 6, 1:00 p.m.

Hello, Ana and Jeff, this is Robert from Guardianship. I really think you're worrying unnecessarily. In our business there is no one hundred percent, but John has rarely been violent. Yeah, I do remember that time he tried to run Jeff over with his car, and the time he went after his roommate with a knife, but that was twenty years ago. John likes to make threats, that's all. I can't say anything positively, but I'm sure your daughter and your grandson are safe. Please call me back.

April 6, 8:00 p.m.

I got your message, you asshole. You're threatening to charge me with harassment? Harassment? You've got your nerve. I know what you're up to, Jeff. You want to charge me with a crime. You want me behind bars. Then you'll get all my money right away. I hate your guts. Why don't you just go suck your cock, Jeff? It's the only thing you're good at.

April 6, 9:00 p.m.

It's Jeanne calling back. Like I said before, you left and I got left with all this shit to deal with. The least you could do is not threaten John. It just gets him all riled up and makes it more difficult for me. Take your phone off the hook and go play golf and sit by the pool or whatever it is you do down there.

April 7, 10:00 a.m.

Hello, Jeffrey. It's your mother. I want to talk to you about harassing John. Please stop. Have a nice conversation with him. Well, okay, then. Good-bye.

April 7, 5:00 p.m.

It's Kim. I got your message, Mom. Yes, I'll make sure the alarm system is on—when we leave and at night. I think during the daytime is a little paranoid, though, don't you? Uncle John is not going to hurt Leo and me. Remember, I'm the one who went to visit him when he was in the care facility.

April 9, 1:35 a.m.
Ana, I woke you up before, didn't I? And you forgot to screen the call. See, I'm very smart. I can outsmart you anytime I want to. You'll have to be on guard all the time. I'll make sure of that. Now, you'll always be wondering if I'm going to call you in the middle of the night. And you can tell my stinking brother I know what he's doing. I'm calling the FBI, the IRS, and the CIA. You are both screwed.

April 9, 1:55 a.m.
Did you think you could go back to sleep? Did you think Johnny would let you alone? You make me want to puke.

April 9, 10:00 a.m.
Hello, Jeff? Ana? Are you there? It's Mom calling. Oh, I wish you'd answer. Pick up the phone so I can talk with you. I talked to John and he won't call you anymore. So don't harass him anymore either. Okay? Oh, I just wish this wasn't happening. I wish it would stop.

April 10, 4:00 a.m.
Here I was thinking I was going to fuck someone tonight, but you must have called and canceled Holly. Can't I even get laid, Jeff? You fuck Ana all the time. Why can't I have a little fun?
I think it's time for another prayer.
Dear God, Please answer my prayers. My brother is going to lose this battle with his life. He will lose this war with John. He will be defeated. My brother is a quitter. He's a quitter and a loser, not a survivor. God, I ask you, please give me victory.

April 10, 11:00 a.m.
Hi, this is Robert at Guardianship returning your call. I'm sorry, Jeff, that you're upset. We're doing the best we can. I'll be in the office until 5:00 p.m. Call me back this afternoon.

April 10, 1:00 p.m.
Mrs. Winston. Please call Calabasas Cardiology as soon as you get this message.

April 10, 2:00 p.m.

Mrs. Winston, this is Rhonda at Calabasas Cardiology. I tried your cell and left a message. Please call us as soon as you get this message.

April 10, 2:15 p.m.

Hi, Dad, it's Kim. I know I didn't talk to you or Mom yesterday, but I had to work late, and then Leo had Open House at school. Lisa from across the street said you called because you were worried. I'm fine. Stop worrying. If it makes you feel better, I will keep the alarm on all the time. Call me later. Love you guys.

April 10, 2:20 p.m.

Mrs. Winston, this is Dr. Martin's assistant at Calabasas Cardiology. We've been trying to reach you. We had to call the paramedics to take Mr. Winston to East Valley Hospital. I can't say more over the phone, but please, go to the hospital immediately. It's urgent.

CLUELESS IN CALIFORNIA

When did thongs start being called flip-flops? Tina wondered as she again tried to pluck the solitary hair from under her chin. The tweezers slipped a little in her grip. Darn, she should have put on the cuticle oil last night, but she'd forgotten. Since her manicure appointment was right before her flight, she'd had to put it on this morning—she needed to soften her cuticles so her nails would look perfect at the reunion. Everything about her had to be perfect tonight—her entire future was riding on it.

She wiped her fingers on a tissue and regripped the tweezers. "Gotcha," she crowed as the hair gave up its roots and released.

Tina continued to examine her face for flaws. "Now people don't hang up their phone, they disconnect," she said aloud. Charlie opened one eye at the sound. He sat at her feet, as he always did, watching her every move.

She looked down at him. "And they don't listen to the radio anymore because they're listening to junk on their cell phones, right? With things sticking out of their ears."

Charlie's meow could have been agreement, or did his shrug mean he didn't care? Well, she did. It bothered her that things got changed without her being aware of it. It made her feel out of touch—made her feel old. And she wasn't. She was in the prime of her life—fifty years old. Well, fifty-three-and-a-half.

She turned to look sideways in the mirror, standing on tiptoe to see as much of her body as she could. She didn't have a full-length mirror any more. Her townhouse, well, two-bedroom condo, didn't have room for one.

She frowned for a moment, thinking of the beautiful home in Beverly Hills she'd been forced to give up. Then she remembered the plastic surgeon had warned frowning could compromise the results of her brow lift. She switched her thoughts to that of a beautiful sunset. She couldn't afford to create a new frown line.

Newly centered, she opened her eyes. By and large, her reflection in the mirror pleased her. Her breasts had always been the bane of her existence—well, at least since seventh grade. She'd felt top-heavy since she was twelve. Then breastfeeding two children and gravity's pull had driven her breasts to her knees. Not a pretty picture in the dating mart. But after her reduction, she was a perky 34 C.

She tore her eyes away from the image of her new-and-improved self to glance at her watch. Oh, God, she was going to be late. Why did everything have to go wrong for her? She rushed around the house, slamming her suitcase shut, and filling Charlie's dishes with enough food and water for the two days she'd be gone.

Two hours later, Tina couldn't believe it when she found a parking place so close to the airport entrance. *Maybe my luck is changing*, she thought as she turned off the engine. She got out of the car and pulled her battered Louis Vuitton suitcase from the trunk. Hitching her carry-on more securely over her shoulder, she rolled her suitcase through the crosswalk and into the terminal. Her eyes filled with tears as she thought about how forlorn Charlie had looked when she'd left. She could easily relate to his feeling of desertion. First her husband, then her two children had deserted her. And most of her friends too.

Up until the time Robert told her he wanted a divorce, she'd felt blessed by good fortune. For twenty years she'd lived a Cinderella life. Then in a flash, it was gone. And Robert, so generous during their married life, turned into a penny-pincher as an ex. Life was just not fair!

Inside, Tina found a long line at the ticket counter. She hadn't checked in online—she hadn't thought she'd needed to.

"My luck," she muttered. She took a deep breath and let it out slowly, just as her yoga teacher had instructed. She began to chant, "Om," in her head, and felt more centered by the time it was her turn.

"Yes? Can I help you, ma'am?" The woman behind the counter looked nothing like an airline employee. More like a kindly grandmother or the old woman who lived in a shoe, Tina thought.

She handed the woman her ticket. "I'm on the Seattle flight at 3:33."

The agent looked at the ticket and then at Tina. "This is for the July 18th flight."

"Yes, I know. Saturday, July 18th."

"Sorry. July 18th was yesterday. Today is Saturday, July 19th."

"What? What are you saying?"

The agent's lined lips thinned. "I'm saying, ma'am, you missed your plane. You're a day late and a ticket short."

What? Did the woman think this was funny? Was it a time for one-liners? The old biddy no longer looked so kindly. Tina clasped her hands tightly, still mindful not to smudge her drying nails. This was not her fault. The computer must have filled in the wrong date.

Panic rose in her throat. She had to be in Seattle by 6:00 tonight. She had to. Her 30th high school reunion began at 7:00 and she had to be there. She'd watched the Dr. Phil show when all those high-school sweethearts had been reunited and fallen in love all over again.

Dieting, working out, and the liposuction had gotten Tina back into fighting form. Now, she was ready to skirmish with her first love. Donald would be at the reunion—she'd checked. He was a dentist in downtown Seattle, so he had to be making big bucks. Sometimes you had to make your own good luck. And though she'd miss the sunshine in California, she was willing to make a sacrifice for a secure future. Anyway, she could always talk Donald into spending time in Palm Springs during the winter.

"Can't I just exchange this ticket for today?"

The ancient agent glanced at the monitor. "Nope, no can do, ma'am. Coach is completely full. The only thing I could do is upgrade you to first class."

"How much would that cost?"

The woman pressed a few keys. "Eight hundred ninety-two dollars one way, ma'am."

"Eight hundred ninety-two dollars? You must be joking. My old ticket was two hundred dollars round-trip."

"That was a special super-saver price." The agent's look conveyed her awareness that Tina was a bargain-basement shopper. "Ma'am, it *is* first class. First class is expensive."

Tina thought about her credit-card limit. She was pretty sure she'd already maxed it out, but it was worth a try. She took a Zen breath and pulled out her wallet. "Okay, here."

The crone took the card. Again she was busy on her computer. Tina stood there, sweating. Her mother always said, "Girls don't sweat, dear.

They perspire." Well, Tina had news for her mother. In Palm Springs, in July, you sweated.

"Ma'am?"

"Yes?" Tina looked at the ticket agent hopefully.

"Your credit card is being denied." The ticket agent smiled, revealing yellowed teeth.

Tina thought about recommending her dentist to the woman. Dr. Waldbaum did a whitening for only $600. She would never let her teeth get to the deplorable shade of the ticket agent's. Once she was married to Donald, she'd be sure to keep up her bleaching. It would be free, after all.

"Do you have another card you'd like to use?" The woman's yellowed teeth gleamed in the artificial twilight of the airport.

"No." Tina was beginning to feel annoyed. She'd chosen this airline because of its television commercial advertising its friendly service. She wasn't seeing any. With her rotten luck she'd probably picked the only unfriendly employee in the entire company.

"Can I speak to your supervisor, please?" Her voice wobbled. She could hear it. So much for the assertiveness-training class she'd spent good money on.

"Sorry, ma'am, he's on break until 4:00."

"But the plane will have already left by then."

"Sorry, ma'am. You'll have to either buy the ticket or step out of line. People are waiting behind you."

Tina turned. Two people, indeed, stood behind her. Both wore expressions of impatience.   "Sorry," she mumbled.

"Ma'am, you need to either give me the correct amount in cash or leave."

Tina pivoted on her heel to face the ticket agent. "You're getting on my nerves. If you call me 'ma'am' one more time in that sarcastic tone, I'll…"

"Are you threatening me?"

"Threatening? You? Me?" Tina didn't shout, but her voice was elevated. At least the ugly biddy was no longer smiling, Tina thought as the woman reached under the counter.

In the next nanosecond, Tina's arm was grabbed from behind. She wrenched away, protecting her purse.

When she turned, she saw a beefy security guard pulling a nightstick from his belt. "Ma'am, you better come with me." His voice vibrated with threat.

"You don't understand. I have to get to Seattle today." She faltered as her eyes filled with tears. She always cried easily, which had angered her as a child. Then she'd found out what a handy tool it could be.

The guard's expression softened. "Why don't you come along with me and explain it." He put away the nightstick and picked up Tina's suitcase.

An hour later, wiping at the tears still streaming down her face, she pushed the automatic door-opener to her garage. She'd turned on the car radio on the way home for company. The announcer had reminded his listeners that it was Saturday, July 19, before reading a news story. If only she'd listened to the radio yesterday morning, she'd have known it was July 18, then. *Why*, Tina wondered, *why do I have such bad luck?*

As she pushed open the door to the house, she found Charlie standing there as if he'd been waiting for her. She picked him up and buried her perfectly made-up face into his fur. "You're a good cat, Charlie Brown. What would I do without you?"

In the kitchen, she took the bottle of Bombay Sapphire out of the freezer. Wiping away fresh tears, she filled a tumbler with gin. She went into her tiny den and flopped onto the couch. Would life ever turn around for her? Would her luck ever change?

Listlessly, she picked up the remote control. People didn't turn on television sets any longer, she thought. No, they clicked it on from across the room. She sighed. Nothing was the same.

She channel-surfed from *Judge Judy* to *Dr. Phil*. She stuck her tongue out at him. "Like I'm ever going to believe one of your shows again." She cast him out of her life forever with a flick of her wrist. She clicked back to *Judge Judy*, took a deep drink from her glass and laid her head back on the pillow.

She had to do something with her life, had to change the way her luck had been running. Maybe she would go to that psychic she'd heard about. It never hurt to take action.

Confessions Of The Hot Flash Queen

So I woke up drenched in sweat, with this pounding headache and a mouth as dry as a used postage stamp. I stumbled to the bathroom for an Extra Strength Tylenol and got a flash of ancient déjà vu. I'd felt like this after drinking bourbon in the back seat of my date's car thirty years ago. But this was no college hangover. No, honey, ready or not, this was Head-On-Menopause.

At the sink, I soaked a washcloth with cold water. I studied my face in the mirror as I wiped it. "Still freckles on white after all these years," I said. "Not too many lines—mostly around the eyes." Smile lines, that's what they were. The one vertical line between my eyebrows had my ex-husband's name written all over it.

Something liquid hit my head. I looked up and took a drop in the eye. Water. As in rain. It was raining again. My roof couldn't take it, and neither could I.

I charged down the hall to my guest room. When I pushed open the door, my worst fears were not denied. The ceiling was weeping right above the crib where my grandson slept on Tuesdays and Thursdays. I shook my fist at the ceiling, at the rain, at Matthew Pierson who was hassling me about the loan for the new roof. It might have been immature, but it made me feel better.

Back in bed, it took me a while to fall asleep. I had an appointment with the loan officer in the afternoon after work. Pierson had been putting me off for no good reason. For me, it was now a matter of triage. I needed that roof, and I needed it now.

Naturally, I woke up late. I threw on a sweatshirt, a pair of jeans, and some Keds. In the kitchen, I poured myself a bowl of organic oatmeal clusters. I ate the cereal without milk. My lactose intolerance level was on high alert. I was even off my three-a-day cappuccino habit. Milk, with or without a moustache, was killing my gut. Maybe that was menopause, too? On the way to work, I had a serious hot flash. Heat flooded my neck and shot upwards. I didn't know I had so many sweat glands on my face. Although it was raining, I rolled down the car window. This was Seattle, so rain reigns. But it was June, and all that Pollyanna, "bright side of needing to use my headlights during a summer day" crap was getting me down. Especially with the deteriorating condition of my roof.

I decided to stop at Expresso-Mio. One cappuccino wasn't going to do me in. The only problem was that five other brainiacs were ahead of me in the drive-thru, and two pulled in right behind me. Since I couldn't get out of line, I turned on the radio to the FM country western station, but even those crooners couldn't calm me down. By the time I got my drink, it was me that was foaming, forget the milk.

I walked into Shear Ecstasy at 9:15. I worked there four days a week doing people's hair. I loved it. Just the smells of shampoos and permanent solution made me happy.

"Hey, Connie, you're barely late," the receptionist called as I passed her desk.

"Yeah, yeah," I said.

I nodded at Susie, my first client of the day. "Be right with you."

"Don't worry. I have plenty of time. Allison's in pre-school all morning."

Susie talked in a voice that was a cross between a Stepford Wife and Marilyn Monroe singing "Happy Birthday, Mr. President". She was one of those forty-somethings who'd decided to retire from Corporate America and have a child to bring meaning to her old age. She was leafing through *Ladies' Home Journal*. Did people still read that?

I put my purse away and slurped up the remainder of my cappuccino.

"I just want a trim," Susie said as I led her back from the shampoo bowl.

Susie's hair was half way down her back. I'd been trying for a year to get her to cut it.

"You know, even the movie stars are getting shorter hair cuts," I said. "I'm not talking Miley Cyrus and buzz cuts, here. But Jennifer Lopez actually has one of those asymmetrical bobs. It's only the extensions that give her the longer look."

Susie looked up from her chamomile tea. "I'm no Jennifer Lopez," she said.

"Hey, no offense intended. You are definitely nothing like Jennifer Lopez."

She's sexy and beautiful, diametrically opposite of you, I thought. But aloud I said, " I don't even know why I mentioned her name."

Sweat broke out on my forehead. I grabbed the magazine out of Susie's hand and started fanning myself. "It must be these hot flashes. I'm sweating so much I'm getting dehydrated and I can't think straight. For all I know, Jennifer Lopez's hair has already grown out and is long again."

I handed the magazine back to Susie. She looked a little apprehensive. Or were the granny glasses just making her eyes look round with fear?

"Maybe I should come back another day," she said.

"How come?"

"You seem a little...a little..."

"Round the bend?" I suggested. "Estrogen deprived? Cuckoo?"

She clutched her purse tighter and nodded.

"Don't worry." I patted her shoulder. "It's really just caffeine deficit. Let me get a cup of coffee, and I'll be my old self."

"Well, if you're sure."

"Not to worry," I said.

Java fortified, I combed out the wet strands of Susie's hair, smoothing it before I began to cut. Doing this never failed to soothe me. I felt the same about freshly sharpened scissors cutting precisely through strands of hair. It was kind of like vacuuming—orderly, and you saw the results right away.

"How come you're smiling?" Susie asked.

"No reason. Just thinking about how much I love my job."

For a moment, the only sound in the salon was loud jazz coming through the speakers. I cut off an inch more of Susie's hair. It definitely needed it.

"I see you've decided to go gray like me," she said.

My eyes met hers in the mirror. "Why would you say that?"

"Gee, did I say something wrong? It's just that you have so much gray showing I figured you were letting your hair go natural."

Not in this lifetime, sister! I moved closer to the mirror and tilted my head. Sure enough, there was a fuzzy caterpillar of gray visible along my part. "Jesus Frango Christ," I muttered. When had that happened? Why hadn't I noticed it? When was the last time I'd had Faye color it?

By lunchtime, I was in a funk. Susie had been gone three hours, her hair four inches shorter than when she came in. I think she said she liked it—that she thought the shorter length would help her night sweats.

I'd had three other clients come in. The last was a teenage boy. His mother had written him an excuse to get out of school so the top third of his black hair could be bleached white blond. It looked funky, but rather skunk-like, too. Hey, I was just there to serve.

Faye, my best buddy who worked on the other side of the salon, had brought me a burrito from next door for lunch. I bit into it and looked at the leftover bleach in the bowl. If I bleached my hair the same as the teenage punker's, my gray wouldn't show so fast.

What did I have to lose? Didn't blondes have more fun? Maybe if I were blond, I'd find a man. Not waiting to assess if I really wanted a man in my life, or if I could stand any more "FUN", I applied the bleach.

Have I mentioned I'm a redhead and have the pale complexion, freckles, and green eyes that go with the syndrome? Gwen Stefani looks swell as a platinum blonde. Me? Not so good. When I was finished, I looked in the mirror. I was white on white. It was like Harry Potter's Invisibility Cloak had dropped over my head.

Only after I'd blown dry my hair did I hear the shriek. From the corner of my eye, I saw Faye running across the salon toward me. Of course, everyone turned to look at her. Did she always have to make a scene?

"Oh, my God. What did you do?" she asked.

"Went blonde?" A quaver ran up and down my tonsils. "Went a little crazy?"

"Oh, my God," Faye repeated. "Why?"

"Why? That's like asking why NASA sends shuttles out into space." I shook my head. "I don't know why. I tried a little at first, and when I liked it, I mixed up a batch and bleached the whole damn thing."

Faye crossed her arms over her chest. "You look like a middle-aged punker. Next thing I know, you'll have your nose pierced. Then how will you go to grandparents' day at Connor's pre-school?"

Faye is a good friend. The only problem is that even though she's younger than I am, sometimes she acts like she's my mother. She stood looking at me, hands on her hips. I had this feeling I was soon going to be put in time-out.

"You fried the ends of your hair," she yelled.

Such outrage over nothing, I thought. Then I peered closer at the mirror. My hair did look like I'd been struck by a medium bolt of lightning.

"I'll have to cut it," I said. "Damn, and it's just grown out to one length."

Faye tapped her toe. "Don't you have that appointment with the loan guy at the bank this afternoon?"

"Oh my God, you're right. With that prissy Matthew Pierson."

I dropped my head into my hands. Even the faint smells of hair bleach and coffee failed to calm me. "I am so screwed."

"Hey, it's not the end of the world," Faye said. "Get a grip."

I lifted my head and looked at her. "You don't understand. The roof is so bad. It's leaking in so many places I can't keep up with it anymore."

Faye put her arm around me. "Just don't take no for an answer from that guy."

"Just don't take no for an answer," I repeated as I waited to see Pierson later that afternoon.

I'd run home, taken a quick shower and changed into a suit. I'd made it to the bank on time, but now I sat cooling my sling-backed heels. I leafed through my folder for a third time. Every objection Pierson had brought up, I'd taken care of. I felt focused. I felt energized. I felt a little too warm.

"Mrs. Bailey?"

I heard my name called, and I jumped. It was Ichabod Crane, the loan officer from hell.

"Hello, Mr. Pierson." I stood up. "How are you?"

"Fine." He smiled at me for the first time in our short history. I hadn't realized he had a space between his two front teeth.

"I barely recognized you. You look so different," he said.

I managed a smile. My heart was beating hard—not a good sign. It meant either a panic attack or a major hot flash was imminent. Maybe in this case, both.

"I really like your hair," Pierson said.

My hair was cut short, real short. By the time Faye had cut off all the split ends, I resembled Mia Farrow when she was married to Frank Sinatra—sort of that neurotic, scarecrow look. Why did Pierson like it? I shuddered to think. And why the hell was he mentioning my hair?

He held my chair for me, also another first.

Still smiling, he went around his desk and sat down. "I'd really like to give you loan approval today," he said. "But there are still two or three sticking points."

"Really?" I crossed my arms. I'd been through this routine with Pierson twice before. What more could have cropped up? "And those are?"

"It's that pesky matter of you having such a new credit rating. You only established it two years ago."

"We've gone through that, Mr. Pierson. That's when I got divorced. I cleared that pesky little matter up with the bank manager," I said. "You were supposed to take care of the forms."

He opened up a folder on his desk and looked at it. "Oh, yes, I forgot."

As he started leafing through the papers in the folder, I realized he hadn't taken the time to prepare for our meeting. My estrogen-deprived body began to heat from the core. I'd had enough of this little pipsqueak.

I stood and put my hands on the edge of his desk. "Listen closely, Mr. Pierson. I'm not leaving here today without that loan. I have taken care of every objection you had. This meeting should just be a formality."

"Please sit down, Mrs. Bailey. Just let me look through the file a minute," Pierson said.

I felt my face flush. "You should have done your homework before I got here. Maybe because I'm a woman needing only a small loan you thought that I wasn't important enough."

Pierson swallowed, sending his Adam's apple into a bobbing frenzy. "Now, Mrs. Bailey…"

"And maybe it's because I'm older, too. That would be two strikes against you. Sexism and ageism."

"Strikes? Sexism and ageism?" Pierson stuttered the words.

I sat back down, and smiled at him. "Two good reasons to sue you and the bank for discrimination."

It was amazing how fast Pierson could get the paperwork done once I pointed out his politically incorrect actions—including complimenting me on my hair.

I ran my fingers through it as I drove home, the loan approval safely on the seat next to me. My platinum white locks were après-hot flash damp again, but who cared? Maybe I could add a little gel and spike it. Maybe even do a faux Mohawk?

Hey, it's all about going with the flow.

Doing Her Best

Late August afternoons can be hot in Seattle, but the hospital cafeteria was chilly. Even the plastic seat of her chair felt cold on Joanna's bare legs. Mac's room faced west and heated up as the sunshine pounded the windows. That's why she dressed in light clothing. Now she wished she'd thought to bring a sweater.

"How's the salad?" Margot asked.

Joanna poked at the wilted greens in front of her. "It's fine, but I can't believe you talked me into coming down here."

"Well, it's almost three o'clock. You said you hadn't eaten anything since breakfast."

"That's true, but I told you I asked the nurse to change Mac's sheets two hours ago. He's been sweating so much, they're soaked through. I know she won't change them, especially if I'm not there."

"Nursing care these days has gone to the dogs. It's disgraceful. But you've got to eat to keep up your strength, Jo. You look so awful. . . like a scarecrow. And your hair. Lord help me, you have grow out everywhere."

Joanna couldn't stop herself from threading her fingers through her hair, but she refused to let Margot's words matter. "There's a lot worse things than gray hair. I've been a little busy. Haven't had time to get to the beauty salon."

"No reason to take offense. I'm worried about you, that's all. And I'm surprised at your tone. You sound so bitter. That's not like you, at all."

Joanna looked at the woman across the table from her. Dressed in her St. John knit suit with her Gucci bag and her perfectly manicured nails, Margot had the sensitivity of a hippopotamus. Usually Joanna could deal with her, but now her patience was at a low ebb. She wanted to slap her.

"Margot, it was really nice of you to stop by the hospital, but as you can see, I'm not very good company. Maybe, you should leave, and I can go back up to Mac's room."

"Absolutely not. You eat that salad. I wasn't kidding when I said you have to eat to keep up your strength. And like I said before, I have something I want to talk to you about. Hold on a minute while I find what I brought for you."

Joanna gave up and took a tentative bite of the dried cheese that topped her salad. It tasted like cheddar flavored plastic.

"Ah, here we are." Margot pulled out a green folder and handed it to Joanna. "This is for you."

"What is it?"

"It's information about the Pacific Northwest Hospice Program. You know, I'm president of the Auxiliary, now." Margot patted her sprayed stiff hair. "They do such an excellent job. Everything you'll need to know is in this folder. I want you to read every one of those brochures."

"Hospice? Why do you think I need to know anything about Hospice?" Joanna dropped the folder as if had been dusted with rat poison. When the radio played an ad for Hospice care, she'd snap it off as quickly as she could.

"Because Hospice knows how to handle situations like yours. I hope you realize what you need to do for Mac at this stage of the game."

"What I realize is that Mac needs positive things to think about if he's going to get well. Hospice is for people who're dying. Mac is *not* dying."

Margot's lips thinned. "See, I knew I needed to talk to you. You don't understand about Hospice. It's for people who are terminal, not necessarily dying immediately."

"Terminal? Dying? What's the difference?" Joanna balled up her paper napkin, and threw it onto her discarded salad. "Don't use those words around me."

"Jo, you're not facing reality. Mac's got pancreatic cancer. Very few beat that."

"You don't know what you're talking about." Joanna's voice shook. "From the very first when we got that damn death sentence--ten months to a year, the doctor said--I made a vow of no negativity around Mac. He and I have always tried our best at everything we do. We've worked hard all our lives and we've succeeded when other people told us we wouldn't. This is no different."

"You're fooling yourself if you really think that."

"No, I'm not. You know Richard Bloch, the CPA who lives on our street? Twenty years ago they told him he only had six months to live. Twenty years ago! And I saw him riding his bike last week. You have to have faith. You have to think positive."

"Did Richard Bloch have pancreatic cancer?"

"I don't know what kind of cancer he had." Joanna shoved the folder back across the table. "I just know he didn't give up, and if I call in Hospice, that's what I'll be doing. I'll be giving up."

Margot leaned forward. "There's giving up and then there's facing reality. You've always been so sensible. I can't believe you're willing to hurt Mac like this."

"How dare you say that to me? I have done nothing but take care of him, made sure he has everything he needs."

"Have you asked him what he thinks he needs, what he wants?" Margot asked. "You need to listen to me. I'm older than you and I've gone through this type of thing before."

"No you haven't. Dale's never been sick a day in his life."

"Not with Dale, but with both of my parents. When my mother got so sick, I didn't want to admit she was going to die, either. But the day comes, when you've got to do what's right."

Joanna clenched her fists as tightly as she could, trying to keep control. Then she swallowed down every swear word she wanted to say. "Don't Margot. Don't you tell me what's right for me. You don't know what's right for me or for Mac."

"I know that you've got to do something. Read these brochures. You can't believe how much Hospice can help you."

"Margot, leave it alone. Mac's been my whole life since I was eighteen. He's my best friend. How can I live without him?"

Joanna shook her head. "I'm not going to do anything that would shorten his life."

"You'll be sorry if you don't do something before it's too late. Take him home to his own bed. Let him be comfortable. Let him be surrounded by his own things."

Joanna pushed back her chair. "Stop it! What are you trying to do to me? I can't give up. I won't give up."

"You're too hard on yourself. You don't have to do this all on your own."

Joanna felt tears welling in her eyes. She'd love to have someone to lean on, to share the pain. But that wasn't possible. She had to be strong for everyone else—for Mac, for the kids.

Margot stood and walked around the table. She put her hand on Joanna's arm. "Go ahead and cry. It's all right."

"No." Joanna shook her head. "I promised Mac I wouldn't cry. It's the least I can do, don't you think?"

"I don't know. I really don't. You're right. I've never gone through anything like this." Margot sighed. "Just look through the folder, that's all I ask."

"All right, Margot. All right." Joanna picked up the Hospice folder. "I'll look at."

"Dianne Rosenberg's card is in there. She's great. Call her or maybe I'll have her call you."

"Please stop. All I said was that I'd read the stuff. That's all I said. " Without another word, Joanna turned and walked out of the cafeteria.

Later, she stood by the window in Mac's room watching a 737 skirt the Space Needle in its descent towards Sea-Tac Airport. No more happy landings for Mac and me, she thought. All my life I've believed that if you're a good person and you work hard, things turn out for the best. There is no best if Mac is dying.

"Mom? What's the matter? Why are you standing over there?"

Joanna turned at the sound of her daughter's voice. "Kimberly, what are you doing here? Don't you have to be at work?"

"It's almost six. I left work a half hour ago."

Joanna looked at her watch. "Time sure flies when you're having fun."

Kim came further into the hospital waiting room. "Where's Dad?"

"Oh, they just took him down for some sort of scan." Joanna stretched and yawned.

"What kind of scan?"

The fear in Kimberly's voice snapped Joanna out of her lethargy. She crossed the room to hug her. "Don't worry. Just some routine check."

"It's more than that. Is Dad worse? Is that why you look so upset?"

"I look upset?"

"Don't try to deny it. Don't try to protect me again." Kimberly pulled away. "I'm twenty-six. I have a right to know everything that's going on. He's my father."

"Of course you do, honey. I respect that. And I've told you countless times that when Dad was diagnosed, I didn't call you because I didn't want to ruin your vacation. There was nothing you could have done here, anyway."

"I don't want to talk about that, Mom. I've already told you how I felt."

Joanna nodded. Yes, Kimberly told her often about her sense of being betrayal.

"It's just been a hard day. To top it off, Margot stopped by."

"Oh? So what kind of trouble did she stir up today?"

Joanna hesitated, unsure of how much she should reveal. But at Kimberly's insistence, she began to tell her about her lunch and Margot's saying that they should take Mac home.

"So she left me that Hospice information." Joanna pointed to the pamphlets sticking out of her purse on the window ledge.

"Throw them away."

"But I promised her I'd read them."

"That woman is just an old busybody. No one's going to make my dad's life shorter, God damn it! Throw them away! No, on second thought, I'll do it myself. Right now."

Kim strode across the room, and grabbed up the pamphlets. She ripped them in half, one by one. "There, that takes care of that."

Kimberly tossed the shredded remains of the pamphlets into the wastebasket, her expression vicious. Its intensity made up Joanna's mind. She felt she was looking into a mirror and it ripped the wrappings off her own blindness. Her own denial.

Mac was dying. That was the truth. The doctors had tried to tell her. Even Mac had been trying to tell her. But she wouldn't listen. Now, she realized how wrong she'd been. She swallowed down the sob building in her chest.

Doing the best for Mac—that was what was important. She fingered the business card of the Hospice co-coordinator in her pants pocket. She'd call her tomorrow.

ERUPTION

"That must be some storm heading this way," Earl said, breaking the silence.

Feigning sleep, I pretended not to hear him. I was so ticked off that if I started to talk to him, I might explode. I needed time to bury my hurt. Goddamn it! Why did he have to be such a jerk to my dad?

I squeezed my eyes closed. I didn't have to say anything if I didn't want to.

As we continued down the highway, the car was unnaturally quiet. The kids were asleep in the backseat, lulled by the late spring heat of Eastern Washington. I'd also turned off the radio several miles back, fed up with the hokey Sunday morning ministers. It was either them or the news shows discussing Jimmy Carter's decision to boycott the Olympics in Moscow. Neither was appealing.

"That must be quite a storm," Earl repeated louder.

This time, I opened my eyes to see what he was so insistent about. The black clouds I'd noticed when we'd turned onto Interstate 90 had not stayed on the horizon, hugging the mountains like they usually did. Instead, they'd fanned out and seemed to be galloping towards us. But did I tell Earl that I could see what he meant? Not on your life. He could tell me the world was round, and I wouldn't agree with him.

We'd just left Spokane after spending a weekend with my parents. Earl, when he hadn't been playing golf or tennis with his college buddies, had argued with my father over anything from politics to who was the best pitcher in the American League.

I shot Earl a dirty look. He'd ruined the trip I'd been looking forward to for months. Since we lived in Seattle, I didn't get to see my parents often.

Even the week before, on Mother's Day, we'd stayed home to be with Earl's mother. I'd had to wait until this weekend to be with my mom. And I'd wanted it to be perfect.

"Mommy, I'm thirsty." Debbie's tone made me want to thump a punching bag. You're seven years old. Stop the damn whining, I wanted to say. Instead, I inhaled the words. The breath I let out probably sounded like the wolf huffing a house down.

"There's a thermos full of water on the seat between you and Jamie. And paper cups in the bag," I said, not turning around.

"But I want a Coke," Jamie said.

I clenched my teeth. Patience, I reminded myself. "All we have is water. So if you are thirsty, drink it."

"Gosh, Mom, you don't have to yell at me."

I turned so I could glare at Jamie, eye to eye. He was ten and into testing me as much as he could. "I repeat—all we have is water."

"Okay, okay." He picked up the brown bag and pulled out a cup. "You want some, Debbie?"

I rolled my eyes. Why couldn't he have been that polite in front of my mother?

Jamie hadn't wanted to come on the trip—he'd had to miss his baseball game. Since he was miserable, he decided everyone else should be, too. He'd done everything in his power to drive Debbie crazy—which led to a fight—which led to me having to discipline and apologize for them. I'd wanted to be a loving mother, but I felt like a drill sergeant with unruly troops.

Sighing for the umpteenth time, I turned back to the front. A few minutes later, I fell asleep for real.

"Jesus Christ, what the hell is going on?"

Earl's words jerked me awake. He sounded frightened. Earl never sounded frightened.

"What—what's the matter?"

"Look up ahead, Eva. Something's wrong. This just isn't normal."

I looked out the window. "Oh my God. You're right. I've never seen anything like that."

While I'd been sleeping, the black clouds had advanced on us even further. Now a line divided the sky between the darkness and the light. "What's happening?"

Earl shook his head. "I don't know, but I don't like it. Not one bit."

I turned to look at the kids. Both were asleep, again, their heads together. They looked so innocent and sweet, nothing like the little sociopaths-in-training they'd behaved like all weekend. Would we be able to protect them from harm?

I shook my head. What kind of storm was heading our way? It had to be a storm, didn't it? What exactly were we going up against?

"Do you think we should turn around?" I asked.

"I don't know if that would do any good. Whatever this thing is, it's coming fast." Earl tapped his fingers on the steering wheel. "Turn on the radio. Maybe we can find out what the deal is."

"Do you think it could be locusts or something like that?"

"Locusts? You think this is Egypt? That it's one of the ten plagues?"

"Oh, great. Sarcasm! That's real helpful." I twisted the radio knob hard. Loud static filled the air between us.

"I wasn't being sarcastic," Earl said. "I was trying to be funny."

"Ha, ha."

He reached over and took my hand. "Honey, I'm sorry. You're right—it wasn't funny. I just don't know what the hell is going on out there. It's making me jumpy. And I got to admit I was already uptight when I got in the car. Trying to get along with your father all weekend was no picnic."

I pulled my hand away. "You call disagreeing with him about everything 'trying to get along'?"

"I didn't disagree with him. He disagreed with me."

"Oh my God. I can't believe you. You're a businessman. You can be so charming with clients. Why not with my dad?"

Earl gave me a sidelong look. "Okay, so I've got at least one thing figured out. That's why you're mad at me. You blame me because your dad treats me like an asshole."

"That is so unfair." I crossed my arms across my chest and looked straight ahead.

Out the window, the cloud was now immense. It streaked across the sky like a thoroughbred horse racing for the finish line. My anger disappeared in a flash.

"Earl, do you see that? The cloud just keeps getting bigger. What is it?"

"I don't know. Don't get freaked out. We're going to get through this just fine." He reached over to take my hand again and squeezed it. "We need to get gas. We'll pull off up ahead and find out what the hell is going on."

He put both hands on the steering wheel and concentrated on his driving. I turned the dial on the radio, trying to find a station, my eyes on the cloud that grew exponentially as we approached it. We were the only car on a freeway that was usually busy, and the radio continued to play only static.

"There's a sign for Ritzville." I pointed it out. "We can get off there."

Earl nodded. We exited the freeway, and I blew out a breath of relief. We'd be okay, now. Once we were in town, we wouldn't feel so alone. There'd be other people who could help us through whatever was happening.

Earl followed the sign to Ritzville's main street. When he turned onto it, my heart almost stopped. The street was deserted.

We cruised past the closed diner, barbershop, and drugstore. The gas station at the end of the road was also closed.

"Shit," Earl said. "What the hell?"

"This is so bizarre. I feel like I'm in the Twilight Zone." I couldn't keep the quaver out of my voice.

"I know what you mean."

He made a U-turn, and we headed back to find the on-ramp. Once we were headed west again on the freeway, I could see how much closer the cloud was.

Earl's concentration on the road was total. On the one hand, I didn't want to disturb him. On the other, I was so scared I wanted to climb into his lap. I bit my lip and decided to keep my growing panic to myself.

Ten minutes later he looked over at me. "Okay, here's the story. I don't know what's going to happen, but that cloud is going to hit us pretty soon. We better get ready."

Ready for what? How did you get ready for something that you have no idea about? I clenched my fists, steeling myself for some kind of impact. But when our car met the cloud, there was no sound, no feel of any collision. We glided smoothly into air, thick with some kind of substance we couldn't identify, but that hadn't created a solid mass.

I turned to check on the kids again. Through the back window of the station wagon, I saw the sunlight ebb away. It was only a little after noon, and we were immersed into darkness.

"Oh, God," I whispered.

"We're going to be fine. We're going to be fine. Don't start to panic." Earl leaned forward to turn on the headlights.

I started thinking about poisonous gases and found I was holding my breath. I let it out, sampling the air, telling myself to stop projecting the worst. "What if there's some kind of chemical poison out there?" I asked.

"We'd already know that by now. It would have come in through the vents, and we'd already be dead."

"Oh." Somehow Earl's terse assessment made me feel calmer.

I looked over at him. My eyes had become accustomed to the dark so I could see his grim expression. His grip was so tight on the steering wheel that his knuckles were white.

"Try the radio again," he said.

"Okay."

For several minutes there was only static, but as we passed by another rural town, the radio picked up a station.

"Thank God." I turned up the volume.

But there was no news, no sermon, no music. "Margaret Millis, your parents want you to stay where you are," the announcer said. "They're safe at Uncle John's." He continued, reading off similar messages. "John Edwards. Grace is with the children at the church."

Earl and I looked at each other. "It must be an emergency broadcast type of thing," he said.

I nodded. "But what kind of emergency? What kind of disaster?"

As we moved on, away from the signal, there was only static again to fill the silence.

My hands started to shake. The only other time I'd been this frightened was when Jamie had been three and had such a terrible asthma attack, he couldn't breathe in the middle of the night. Then, I called 911. The medics were at our house within five minutes. Now we were alone.

"Hey, cool. Look how dark it is. Mount St. Helens musta blew!" Jamie leaned over the back seat, his head between Earl and me.

"Say that again, Jamie."

"You know, Mom, Mount St. Helens. You know how they were predicting it was going to erupt anytime."

"Oh, my God. Of course, Mount St. Helens."

Earl caught my eye. "Jesus, what's the matter with us? What were we thinking?"

I shook my head. "Too caught up in other things?" I didn't voice the rest of my thought—too caught up in fighting about our parents.

"Mommy, is it nighttime?"

"Oh, Debs, you're awake, too, sweetie?"

"Yep. Why is it so dark?"

"It's the ash from the volcano, Dorko."

"Jamie, don't call your sister a dork." I turned to frown at him. Although he looked like an angel while he slept, as soon as he was awake, devilment danced in his eyes.

"But you said, Mommy, that the mountain is so far away that it could never hurt us."

"I know, Debbie. It's true. We're going to be fine."

"Yeah, but my science teacher said that when the volcano erupts, it'll blow its top clean off."

"Jamie, sit back in your seat and put on your seatbelt," Earl ordered.

"Okay, okay. But I'm telling you—Mr. Morton said the ash could be spread for thousands of miles if the particles get into the upper atmosphere."

"I doubt that, Jamie. Stop trying to scare your sister," I said.

"Yeah, stop trying to scare me."

"Ouch. Mom, Debbie hit me."

Sweet and innocent? Sure they were. "You kids be quiet. Dad needs to concentrate."

"Your mother is right. I can barely see the highway. So stop screwing around back there."

"Okay, Daddy. Sorry."

"We don't want to scare you, but Daddy and I aren't kidding. This is worse than when it's foggy so you, two, need to be on your best behavior."

"Okay, Mom. We hear you. We'll be good, right Debs?"

"Right." I heard the edge of fear back in her voice.

The car, for the second time that day, became unnaturally silent—the only sound the wipers rasping against the gritty specks on the windshield. But as we traveled further into the cloud, the wipers didn't do much good. The ash was thicker and stuck to the glass as if glued. One good thing—at least we weren't alone anymore. I could see cars' taillights ahead of us.

"We're getting off the highway," Earl said a few minutes later. "It's too dangerous. I can't even see to drive."

His back rigid with tension, he leaned forward to peer out the windshield. "I want to try to get to that Rest Area near here. I know it's close."

We began to inch our way forward. It seemed like forever before Jamie called out, "There's the exit sign for the Rest Area." His sharp eyes had picked out the sign barely visible through the gloom.

We crawled down the ramp, Earl steering on the slippery surface as if we were on black ice. The lot was crammed full of cars, but he made his own place at the end. He put the car into park and shut off the engine.

"Thank God," he said. He wiped perspiration from his forehead. "We're safe now."

I wondered if he were right. Although it was only one o'clock in the afternoon, the volcanic ash had leached the light from the day. The cars in the lot cast shadows around us, making me feel as if our doom had been sealed. We had no idea how long the air would remain so densely filled with ash. Would we be marooned here for long? We had little food with us, and not a lot of Jamie's medication, either.

"I have to go to the bathroom."

"Debbie, you shouldn't have drank so much juice at Grandma's," Jamie said.

"Don't start bickering again, you guys," Earl put in before Debbie could reply. "We still have major problems."

"Yes, you two. We all need to cooperate to get through this." I gave them each the "no nonsense or you're grounded for life" look. "Jamie, do you need to go to the bathroom, too?"

"Nah, not me. I'm not the one who drank a lot of juice."

"I'm so glad you're not going to antagonize your sister." Earl's tone was dry.

"Is antagonizing bickering?" Jamie asked as if he really wanted to know.

Earl ignored him. "Eva, you take Debbie, and I'll stay with Jamie. When you get back, I'll go use the pay phone and see what I can find out."

"That sounds like a plan. Come on, Debs, let's go."

"Take the flashlight," Earl said.

"Good idea." I opened the glove compartment. "We should probably use an umbrella, too. It should help keep the ash off of us."

"Good idea." Earl turned toward the backseat. "Jamie, get Mom the umbrella in the back."

After Jamie handed me the umbrella, I opened the door. "Hurry, Debbie. The ash is getting inside the car."

We found the bathroom with no trouble, used it, and were back at the car within ten minutes. The only problem was that we were covered in ash. The umbrella had shielded us, but not completely. It had been hot in Spokane when we'd left, so Debbie and I wore only halter-tops and shorts. The ash lay on our skin like sand. At least it didn't burn. What if it had been acidic?

I brushed at Debbie's shoulders. What kind of mother was I? Why hadn't I thought of any of this before? I knew that the volcano was supposed to erupt. I knew Jamie could have breathing problems if it did. I'd even bought him some of the paper masks they'd been advertising. They were at home, though, safely tucked away in the pantry. A lot of good they'd do us.

Earl rolled down the passenger window "Why are you doing standing out there?"

"We've got ash all over us. I'm trying to brush Debbie off."

"I'd just get into the car. By the time you're finished, she'll be covered again."

"I guess you're right." I turned to Debbie. "I'm going to have you get in front with me. I'll try to clean us off when we're in the car."

"Okay, Mom." She nodded and then coughed.

I looked at her in alarm. If she were going to have problems breathing because of the ash, what would happen to Jamie? He got an asthma attack from the slightest amount of pollution.

I opened the door, scooted in, pulling her with me. When the door was closed tight, I let out my breath. The air stirred some of the ash. This time I coughed.

My throat felt clogged. I bent over at the waist, coughing, trying to clear it.

"Are you okay, Eva?" Earl's voice was filled with concern.

"Yeah, Mom, are you okay?" Jamie repeated. He leaned over the seat to look at me.

I nodded. When I tried to sit up, I began to cough again. I returned my head to my knees.

I coughed once more, hard, and felt the constriction in my throat ease.

"That was scary," I said when I could sit up.

"That's an understatement." Earl's thumb traced my cheekbone with a gentleness I didn't know he possessed.

Then he straightened his shoulders. "I'm going to go use the phone. I'll try to find out how long we'll be here."

"Put on your sweatshirt with the hood. That should give you better protection."

His jaw tightened. He liked to give directions, not take them.

"Good idea," he finally said.

He turned toward Jamie. "Climb in the back. I think my sweatshirt is in my duffle, which should be near the door."

"Sure, Dad." In the gloom, Jamie all but disappeared into the back of the station wagon. "Got it," he called.

"Just hand me the sweatshirt. Leave the duffle there," Earl ordered.

Couldn't he say please? I wondered.

But Jamie didn't seem to notice his father's lack of manners. He sailed the shirt to the front of the car. "Okay. Here it comes."

Earl caught it. He put an arm through a sleeve and pulled the sweatshirt over his head. "Thanks."

"No problemo," Jamie said. He climbed over into the backseat.

"While you're gone, I'll try to get us cleaned up and organized," I said.

"Good." Earl started to open the car door, but then turned to look at me. Rarely had I seen his expression so serious.

"I just want to tell you I love you." He spoke so quietly I had to lean over to hear him. "I know I don't say it often enough."

"Thank you. I love you, too."

"I've just been thinking." He swallowed hard. "It's pretty damn good that I know I can always depend on you."

"And I can always depend on you—unless there's some game on the tube."

He laughed as I'd intended, gave me a quick kiss, then ducked out his door. He was so quick that almost no ash filtered into the car. That was Earl, a man of action—not of words. I smiled. That made what he'd just said especially precious.

"Hey, Mom, is this cool or what?" Jamie, who'd surprised me by not making gagging noises when his father kissed me, put a paper cup in front of my face.

"What's inside?" I asked.

"Ash. I collected it."

"Really? Where?" I swivelled so I could see him.

"I rolled down the window and stuck my hand out."

"Jamie!"

"What's wrong with that, Mom?"

"Didn't you hear how Debbie and I were coughing?"

"Yeah, so what?"

"We don't have asthma, and we're coughing, that's so what. You've got asthma. You get ash in your lungs, and it won't be a pretty sight."

I frowned at him. "We're trying to protect you, here. It's bad enough that Debbie and I have ash all over us and brought it inside. Our goal is to keep the ash out, not bring it in. Don't put your window down again."

"Aw, Mom. Every time I'm having fun, I have to stop because of asthma."

"Yeah, well, that's the breaks, kiddo. You play with the hand you're dealt."

He made a face at me.

I made an equally hideous one at him. He tried to keep from smiling, but he couldn't.

I smiled back. "You were so good at finding Dad's sweatshirt. Would you like go on another search and rescue mission?"

"I guess."

"I'll do it, Mommy."

I looked down at Debbie, still glued to my side. "Hey, you sure have been quiet."

"Well, everyone's been so busy talking so fast, I couldn't find a side road to get a word in."

I laughed and hugged her. "As soon as you're cleaned off, you can get in the back and help Jamie with what we need."

It took us about 20 minutes to get everything set. While I wiped Debbie down with paper towels, I directed Jamie to get his medication from his suitcase, along with a long sleeved shirt and pants, and then to look for warmer clothes for all of us. In the darkness, the air was much cooler than it had been when we'd set out.

I sat on my knees in the front seat, facing the kids. "Here's a Theopholin tablet, Jamie. Pour yourself some water from the thermos and take it."

"Why do I have to take this junk?" He rubbed his eyes. "I haven't had asthma for a long time."

"It's just a precaution, honey. This ash is tough on everyone. Remember how I was coughing a little while ago?"

"Yeah, yeah." He poured himself some water. "These are so big, I can barely swallow them."

"I know. But you do it anyhow." I tousled his hair.

"I wonder when Daddy's going to be back?" Debbie was settled into her corner of the backseat with the two Barbie dolls my mother had given her.

"It won't be long," I said.

By the time Earl returned, Barbie One and Barbie Two were fighting over who was going to wear the only pair of stiletto heels in their combined wardrobes. I was getting ready to shoot myself or tear the dolls limb from limb.

As Earl slid behind the wheel, fine grains of the gray ash filtered into the car with him. He pulled his sweatshirt over his head, rolled it a ball, and put it at his feet, next to the umbrella. "I got through to everyone," he said.

"What did they say?"

"My dad's playing golf, and my mom didn't even know the mountain had erupted."

Typical, I thought, his parents are absolutely clueless. "How about my folks?"

"Your mom said, 'Thank God' and then started asking if we had enough to eat and drink. She kept saying she usually gave us a lot of food to take home, but she hadn't because we were in such a rush to leave. That's when your dad took the phone."

"What did Dad say?"

Earl looked at his hands on the steering wheel. "I think your dad might have been crying. He kept saying, 'I'm so glad to hear your voice. I'm so glad to hear your voice.'"

He met my gaze. "I think he meant it—that he was glad to hear my voice—that I was okay, not just you, not just the kids."

"He does care about you, you jerk. I told you that."

"Yeah, I guess you were right." Earl raised his eyebrows. "Who knew?"

I laughed and brushed at my front. More ash particles swirled around us.

Earl let out a sigh. "This car is going to be a mess."

"Like it already isn't?" I made the same face at him as I had to Jamie.

"Jesus! You better hope the ash doesn't freeze your face like that."

I laughed. "It could come in handy dealing with the men in my life."

"Are we that hideous?"

"I'm taking the fifth on that." I leaned over to brush some ash off his face. "What did you find out about the eruption?"

"Your dad said they announced on the news that the mountain is quieting down. We should be able to get moving soon."

"That's good news. Hey, you guys. Did you hear that? We can leave soon."

"I'm hungry," Debbie answered.

"Me, too," Jamie said.

"Well, let's eat then."

After we finished the lunch I'd packed, Earl encouraged us all to take a nap.

"I don't take naps anymore, Daddy," Debbie said. "I'm six."

"I know how old you are. I'm thirty-six and I'm taking a nap. We'll go use the restrooms, and then we're all taking a nap."

Like the good soldiers we were, we followed his orders.

Jamie's cough awakened me. I peered at my watch. It was already five o'clock. "Oh my God, I can see the dial without any problem!"

Earl stirred next to me. "What are you yelling about?" He stretched and yawned.

"It's so much lighter out. The ash must not be as thick."

"Hey, you're right. I can see the car next to me." He leaned over and turned the key in the ignition.

"Where are we going?" I asked.

"Nowhere. I just want to listen to the radio without using the battery." He flipped the radio dial up and down with a rapidness that made me dizzy. Finally, he tuned into a station.

"The mountain has stopped erupting," the newscaster announced.

"Thank God," I said.

Jamie started coughing in the backseat. Earl turned up the volume.

"We're not out of the woods yet, folks." The newscaster sounded like he was giving the play-by-play of some ball game. "Scientists are predicting another explosion, perhaps as soon as within three hours."

I turned to Earl. "What are we going to do?"

"I want to try to get back to Spokane."

"I don't think it's a good idea."

"Eva, we just can't sit here. You said you only have two more tablets for Jamie, and we're all going to be hungry soon. Look, other cars are leaving." He pointed out the window.

I bit my thumb. "But the road was so slippery before."

Earl put the car in gear, his motion jerky. "Have a little confidence in me, for God's sake."

"Okay. I will—I mean I do."

We inched our way out of the parking lot, the ash under the tires just as slippery as earlier. As we passed a van, our car slid toward it, but Earl spun the wheel to steer us away at the last minute.

On the highway, the conditions were even worse. Ash swirled around us—not new ash, but what had already accumulated—stirred up by the movement of the cars. It cascaded at window height, obscuring our sight. Again I felt encapsulated in a black fog.

I closed my eyes. Oh my God, I thought. We're never going to make it back to Spokane. We could die out here. Oh my God. Oh my God.

"What the hell. There's more ash inside the car. Where the hell is it coming from?"

My eyes flew open. A dusting of undisturbed ash lay on the dashboard. Sweat trickled down my forehead. If a lot of ash started coming into the car, what would happen to us?

"Shit. Shit. Shit." Earl started flipping dials on the dashboard.

"What? What's wrong?"

"It's the air filter system. The ash is being sucked in through the goddamn air filter system."

"Oh, no." I leaned forward to close the vents on my side, fumbling with the lever.

"Daddy's going to owe the swearing box a lot of money," Debbie said to Jamie in the backseat.

I almost laughed. Never underestimate Debbie's ability to see the entire picture, I thought to myself. Her perspective calmed me. I took a deep breath. I couldn't fall apart—couldn't let the fear overtake me. We had to protect these kids. That was the bottom line. I gritted my teeth. Why hadn't we stayed at the Rest Area? At least it was safe there.

"Closing the vents helped," Earl said a few minutes later.

"Yeah, but it was like closing the barn door after it's too late." I shot him a look. "You couldn't leave well enough alone, could you? You had to get back on the highway. You always have to do everything your way."

He banged his hand against the steering wheel. "If you don't have anything constructive to say, just don't say anything."

"Mommy, Daddy, don't fight." Debbie's voice was so quiet, I almost didn't hear her over Jamie's coughing.

I unclenched my fists. "Okay, Debbie, you're right. Daddy and Mommy won't fight." Fighting would only waste our energy, and we needed to conserve it.

As I sat looking out the windshield, seeing nothing but a faint reflection of myself in the glass, I realized that my own chest felt tight again. All of us were going to choke on the ash if we couldn't get a handle on it. Then I remembered the paper towels. Where had I put them? I reached down in front of me. When I felt the softness of the roll, I gave a little prayer of thanks.

"Okay, everyone, I'm going to give you each a paper towel." I handed one to Earl, and then turned to the back to give them to the kids. "Put the towel over your mouth. It should act as a mask and help us breathe better."

No one argued with me, which was a first.

We continued down the highway, driving no more than ten miles an hour. Periodically, Earl stopped the car to let the ash outside settle around us. Jamie's wheeze worsened as we struggled to make progress down the road. I climbed over the seat to the back and had Debbie move to the front. First I gave Jamie another pill. Then I pulled him close and began massaging his back. He relaxed against me—his breathing eased somewhat.

I looked out the window to avoid answering the questions I saw in his eyes. Something loomed, ghostlike to our right. "Could that be the Ritzville sign?"

"I hope to God it is," Earl said. "Yes, I think you're right. I can see some lights."

I leaned back against the seat, hopeful again. If we could just get into town, we could find someone, somewhere, who could tell us how to get to a hospital. Jamie needed a shot of adrenaline, needed it as soon as possible.

Earl began to maneuver down the exit, going slowly so he wouldn't have to apply the brakes. The car's engine sputtered.

"Now what?" I asked.

Earl shook his head. "Maybe the ash is getting into the engine and clogging it?"

"That would be a disaster."

Earl said nothing in reply.

Halfway down the exit, visibility again dropped to almost zero. The lights we'd seen disappeared into thin air.

"Shit. I can't see a goddamn thing. I wonder if I should pull over?"

Earl's question was soon moot. The engine shuddered once and stopped. The car kept sliding down the exit like a sled on a snow-covered hill, gaining speed as it went. Earl had to apply the brake—he had no choice. The car fishtailed. It hit the railing, ricocheted off of it, then back into it. After what seemed like an eternity, it stopped.

There was total silence for a moment. Then Debbie's plaintive voice filled the air. "Daddy, are we going to live?"

"Yes, Debbie, of course." Earl's voice, usually so full of abrupt energy, held a soothing quality. It scared me to death.

He tried to start the engine. Nothing.

"I'll let it sit for a while," he said. "Maybe it's flooded."

In a few minutes, he tried it again. Nothing.

"What should we do? Jamie's breathing is getting worse. We need to get him to an emergency room." I tried to keep the fear out of my voice, but I didn't do a very good job of it.

"I could go for help, but I'm afraid I wouldn't be able to find you again." Earl turned to look at me in the backseat. "Remember I saw a lot of lights ahead? Let's get out and walk a little ways. We shouldn't be far from the center of town."

"Go out in that ash? That's crazy. I don't want Jamie out there." I shook my head. "I don't want any of us out there."

"Eva, for Christ's sake, be practical. We have to get out. Our car is in a terrible place to begin with. We have no choice. So, let's get moving."

"Just like that you're issuing orders? Maybe you could ask my opinion and listen to it for once."

Earl rounded on me. "Sorry, Miss Manners, if I don't have the time to be polite. We are in the middle of a disaster here."

I glared at him. "I get it, but you don't have to act like a damn dictator."

"I'm not acting like a dictator, goddamn it!"

His shoulders sagged. "I'm sorry for coming on so strong. And I wish to hell I was doing a better job of protecting you. I don't even have a goddamn compass."

"Dad sounds so upset," Jamie whispered.

I nodded and kissed the top of his head.

"Earl." I put my hand on his shoulder and squeezed it. "It's not all up to you. We're in this together. We're going to figure it out. But, honey, we need to feel like we're a team. We need to discuss what we're going to do."

"Okay. I see your point." He sat straighter and his eyes met mine. "So let's talk. I think we need to get out of the car and walk toward where we saw the lights. What do you think?"

I stared at him. Now that he'd asked for my opinion, I froze. I'd always believed I was protected in some way—that disasters happened to people who lived in dangerous places, not to someone like me. Now, I felt as if the earth had shifted, and my place of balance was off-kilter. I still wished we were back at the Rest Area, but there was no point in dwelling on what could have been. We were here, sitting in a stalled car in the middle of an off-ramp. We had to get out.

"All right. Let's do it."

Earl smiled. "Good decision."

"I think we should put on another layer of clothes for protection," I said.

"Good idea."

"I'll climb in back and get the clothes out, Dad," Jamie offered.

"I'll help you," I said. "And move slowly, okay. Your lungs are already working overtime."

"Sure, Mom."

"What can I do, Daddy?"

"Well, Debs, let's see." Earl paused. "I know. Take that roll of paper towels and pull off the pieces. That way, we can each put some in our pockets."

Once we were ready, we opened the doors and got out. Earl locked the door. "Like it matters," he said under his breath.

He took Jamie's arm. I held onto Debbie with one hand. In the other, I held the umbrella over our heads.

Earl shone the flashlight on the ramp as we began to walk down it. We couldn't see much through the ash, but the diffused beam made it feel we weren't walking blind. Even so, our progress was slug-slow, hampered by the ash that came up to Debbie's knees.

She slipped, and her hand wrenched out of mine as she tried to right herself. Dropping the umbrella, I caught her before she fell. I drew her to my side to steady her, my heart thumping in my chest. I held onto her, afraid I'd lose her as I had once in a nightmare.

"Here, let me carry Debbie. The ash is too deep for her," Earl said. The paper towel over his mouth muffled the words. "Jamie, you walk with Mommy under the umbrella."

He lifted Debbie and she put her arms around his neck.

"All right. Let's think this through. We know this ramp will take us to a street. We know we were driving east. If we turn right, we'll be going south." Earl looked down at Jamie. "You're the one with the great sense of direction, Jamie. I'm going to need your help keeping us straight. All right?"

A small smile played across my lips. Earl was trying hard to include us all in the decision making process.

"Sure, Dad." The words threw Jamie into a paroxysm of coughing.

Earl and I stood there, staring at each other, listening to the cough and the wheeze beneath it.

"He needs a hospital. He needs adrenaline," I said.

"I know. That's why we have to keep moving."

"Yes, that's the reason." I put my arm around Jamie. "Let's go, sweetie. Lean on me."

We walked on. Except for the sound of Jamie's labored breathing and the swish of the ash as we shuffled through it, it was as quiet as if we were in outer space.

We finally reached the bottom of the ramp. "Okay, this is where we turn right," Earl said.

Jamie's cough continued as he struggled to walk beside me, his head down. The transformation from his normal irrepressible self to this stumbling child made me want to cry. But I'd have to save that luxury for later. My focus was on one thing only—keeping moving, one step at a time.

"Stop a minute," Earl said after a while.

I glanced at him. "Why?"

"Do you think you can take Debbie? I'll carry Jamie. He can't walk anymore."

"You're right" I held out my arms. "I can carry her."

At first, I staggered under her weight, but I regained my balance. She held me tightly, which also helped. Her head so close to mine, I could hear her whimper.

"It'll be okay, sweetheart. Mommy's got you. We're going to be all right. You'll see."

Earl lifted Jamie. "Let's walk close together—try to keep the ash from moving so much."

I nodded. "Good idea. I wonder how much further we have to go?"

"I don't know." Earl sounded exhausted.

I squared my shoulders. "Well, however far, we'll just keep going. Right?"

"Right." He leaned over to kiss me. I kissed him back.

"Together, we'll make it," I said.

We started walking side by side, not talking, saving our strength. One step at a time, I repeated to myself. It became a mantra.

"Eva?" Earl called my name, bringing me back to the dark. "Eva! I think I see lights up ahead."

I looked up. " Oh my God, I can see them, too."

Earl eased Jamie to the ground. "Lean on me, son."

I stopped, too, and put Debbie down.

Earl raised the flashlight over his head, waving it in an arc. First he did it quickly, then, as the lights moved closer, more slowly.

Through the haze of ash, I could see two distinct lights now. "It's a car," I said. "Oh my God, it's a car."

As it approached, I could see it was a police car. We didn't move from our spot—we just let it come to us. When it stopped, an officer opened the driver's door and got out.

"You people having some trouble, looks like," the man said.

"Our son has asthma. Our car stopped and . . . "

"That's all right, now. You can tell me all about it later. Let's get you all in the car and get that boy to the hospital. The mountain erupted again, and there's no telling what's going to happen."

Without another word, we followed him to the car. We four sat huddled close together in the backseat, glued together by our tension. It had been just us out there—our world had narrowed to the four of us. It was difficult to accept we weren't alone anymore.

I don't know how long we'd been in the car when Jamie started gasping for air. Earl took him on his lap.

I felt I had to hold myself very still to keep Jamie safe—that if I moved, the pieces of the jigsaw puzzle we'd found to keep us alive would scatter—that Jamie might not survive.

"Don't worry. We're almost there. I'm going to radio them so they'll be ready for us," the officer said.

When we drove into the parking lot of the hospital, it was so pitch dark, the lights were barely visible. "We would never have found it if the policeman hadn't brought us," I whispered to Earl.

"I know." His voice rasped like a rusted saw.

The policeman pulled up in front of the emergency entrance. Two attendants came rushing out, pushing a gurney.

Earl opened the car door and helped Jamie out. "I'm going to lift you up onto this rolling bed," he said.

"Here, I'll help you." One of the attendants reached forward.

Together, they lifted Jamie onto the gurney.

By that time, I stood next to them. A woman in a white coat, a stethoscope around her neck, had also joined us. She placed an oxygen mask over Jamie's mouth and nose. He could breathe now—and so could I.

The woman looked up from adjusting the oxygen tubing. She stared at us as if we were apparitions. "I'm Dr. Mandlekorn. I'm a pediatrician helping out here. Your son is going to be fine, now."

"He needs adrenaline," I said.

She smiled. "I agree. We're going to take him inside, give him adrenaline, and get him onto an IV drip." She paused and then pointed to the tall, thin attendant. "I'd like you to give Michael, here, a quick health history."

"I'll follow you inside and give you the information," I said.

The attendant, Michael, put up a hand. "No, ma'am, you're covered in ash. We can't let you in."

"But I'm his mother. I have to go with him."

I felt a hand on my shoulder. I looked around. Earl, holding Debbie, had moved to stand by my side. "Yes, we're his family. We have to be with him," he said.

"We'll take care of him. He's safe now, believe me." Dr. Mandlekorn's voice was calm. She looked me in the eye and then turned to Earl. "You go with the officer. He'll take you to the Red Cross care station. They'll vacuum you off and get you something to eat. Then come back."

Earl looked down at me. "What do you think?"

I put my arm around his waist. "I think we have to do what they say. We have to trust them."

He thought for a moment and then nodded. He turned to the doctor. "We're leaving him in your hands for now."

"Thank you." She started to leave and then turned back. "I just want to say that I think you are all so brave. I don't know if I could have survived out there."

"What do you mean?" Earl asked.

"I heard over the CB that Officer Rasmussen found you out in the middle of a road—the four of you, standing together—covered with ash. It had to take a lot of courage to keep going."

Earl shrugged his shoulders. "We just did what we had to do. That's all."

I leaned into him. "We're a good team," I said.

"And how." Earl winked at me.

Debbie raised her head from his shoulder. "I'm part of the team," she said to the doctor.

"She sure is. We all did this together. We all helped," Earl said.

My eyes filled with tears. How lucky we were. Out in that ash storm, we'd found more than just our safety. Through my tears, I smiled at Earl—then I began to laugh.

"What's so funny?"

"You look like a huge, gray Bigfoot. Ash is definitely not your color."

"You wouldn't win a beauty contest, either, sweetheart. Not with those tears running down your face. You look like a zebra."

He tweaked my nose. Ash drifted off it. "Come on, let's go get cleaned up."

HER FATHER'S DAUGHTER

Emily picked up the steak knife next to her plate. Instead of an eating utensil, it looked promising as a weapon. Her mother had just ordered ketchup to go on her salmon. But Mother didn't call it ketchup.

"Bring me some *catsup*," she told the waiter as if she were the queen of England ordering the finest béarnaise sauce. The word ketchup was way too déclassé for momma dearest, but dumping tomato crap over the salmon was okeydokey.

Emily replaced the steak knife on the damask tablecloth. Stabbing her mother in the middle of Wally's was not a real option. It would have caused a sensation, though. Wally's was an old jewel of a restaurant in Palm Springs, where her parents spent the winter. The patrons, those still actually breathing on their own, would have gasped at the attempted matricide.

Emily's mother sat at the head of the table, her posture erect, her nose pointed ceiling-ward. Mother did remind Emily of Queen Elizabeth in many ways. Both looked like they'd never uncrossed their ankles in their lives, but each had four kids. That meant they'd had sex at least four times. Emily knew this because she no longer believed that Jesus was the true Son of God. Ergo, the doctrine of Immaculate Conception was kaput. Which left the world with the inconvertible existence of eight children—four of them living in castles in England close to their mother, Elizabeth II, and four living all over the United States as far away from their mother, Helene Moore, as possible.

Emily herself still lived too close, but her husband's company was based in Sacramento, so that's where they had to be. That put her at Helene's beck quite often. Last week her mother had wanted a particular stamp for her holiday cards. Emily, after a full day of counseling unhappy teens, and in between driving Henry and Leo to football practices, detoured to the post office so her father wouldn't have to. That was Helene's real hold on Emily. Ever since Daddy's heart attack, Emily tried to protect him from aggravation. The result? She was in the vermillion-tipped talons of her mother's power.

Emily looked around the table. All four of the Moore progeny were partaking of a meal together for the first time in years to celebrate their father's 75th birthday. Daddy sat next to Mother, his shoulders slightly hunched. Emily smiled at him. His return smile was brief and didn't reach his eyes. He quickly looked away from her. Emily frowned. What was up with that?

She wondered if he was worried about G-G and Doc. Her grandparents were in their late nineties. Normally they would have flown to Palm Springs for this occasion, but Doc had a cold, and decided to stay home. Emily had thought G-G might come, but at the last minute, she canceled. Her grandparents had been fighting a lot lately. Emily thought about the knock-your-socks-off phone call she'd received from her sister.

"Are you sitting down?" Lauren had asked.

"No, but I will if you insist," Emily said.

"Suit yourself. Here's the news. G-G wants a divorce."

Emily sat down. "A divorce? They've been married for over seventy-five years. They can't get divorced."

"G-G says she's sick and tired of Doc telling her what to do all the time."

"You'd think she would have spoken up in the first fifty or sixty years," Emily said.

"She told me Doc won't let her breathe. The direct quote was: 'Pretty soon I'll have to buy air so I'll have some to breathe.'"

"Yikers," was the only comment Emily had come up with.

"We drove over four hundred kilometers into the wilds of Canada this summer. You wouldn't believe all the bears we saw," Scott, Emily's oldest brother said, bringing her back to the present. His voice dictated attention, even if his speech now was slurred by the third, or was it fourth, glass of merlot.

He was ten years older than she, and looked every one of his 53 years, Emily thought. The big clue was the cliffhanger stomach, cinched by a belt taxed to its limit. Or maybe it was the bags under his eyes.

"Up at Whistler Mountain, you had to take a bell with you on a hike. You'd shake it every once in a while to let the bears know you were coming. It was supposed to scare them away," Annabella, Scott's wife, said. She was newly wife number two, tall, blond, and a great golfer. Emily had discovered the last fact during the afternoon. They'd played their Moore family tournament and Emily had been paired with Annabella. Besides the fact that Annabella out drove her (and half the men), could hit out of any sand trap, and putted lights out, Emily had liked her. Especially compared to Patricia, wife number one.

Mother had been devastated when Scott and Patricia split up. "Why, she was one of the best presidents Junior League ever had," Mother said, as if that compensated for Patricia's personality and lack of integrity. Emily thought her ex-sister-in-law was a bigger snob than Mother and even more negative. Patricia had thrown a fit just because Emily had worn her "Obama Hope" T-shirt to the country club one afternoon.

"I thought this was a free country," Emily said when Patricia insisted she change.

"First of all, your shirt doesn't have a collar and you know that's against the rules. And second, promoting that liberal in front of all my friends is not going to happen," Patricia had hissed.

Emily was still sorry about that. She'd seen all the McCain stickers on the Mercedes and Jaguars in the parking lot, and had been looking forward to the feedback she'd get walking to the swimming pool. She'd complied because Scott would have killed her back then. Scott liked the country club and Patricia's pedigree just fine; it was her predilection for muscled tennis pros that had broken up the marriage.

"Would you like another martini, ma'am?" the waiter who'd appeared by Emily's side asked. She looked up at him. "I'll just have a Coke."

"Pepsi all right?" he asked.

"Sure," she said. She didn't like Pepsi, but she was the designated driver tonight so she'd make do.

She listened as her husband agreed to his third vodka on the rocks. Since the economy had tanked, Daniel got tanked quite often. His company had been hit hard and he was now back on the road. Emily was worried about Daniel, what the stress was doing to him. When she tried to bring it up, he snarled at her. They'd been such a close family once—done everything together, but now Daniel shut them all out. Three years before, he'd been Leo's baseball coach. Now he rarely made it to a game.

She could feel Daniel's leg jiggling next to hers. She put her hand on top of his thigh.

"What?" he asked, pulling away.

"Just wanted to say I love you," she whispered.

Picking up the drink the waiter had set in front of him, he took a swallow and said nothing.

Emily was astonished to feel tears burn in her eyes. She'd expected their usual response to each other: *Love you too*. It was almost a throwaway line, but now that he hadn't said it, she realized its strength in connecting them as a family. She wasn't the sentimental sort, really didn't need a lot of attention. But Daniel's continued coldness was getting to her. She'd been able to count on him, count on their family's unity as her compass. Now she didn't know where she stood.

She turned away from him to her brother Connor. He lived in Alaska and had come to Palm Springs by himself. His wife, Colleen, was a teacher and said she couldn't get the time away. Emily suspected the truth was that Colleen couldn't take another session with Queen Helen, who never missed the opportunity to comment on Colleen's plainness.

"Your hair is so full of gray—so drab. Why in heaven's name don't you color it?" Mother had asked Colleen at Daddy's 72nd birthday.

That celebration had been in Hawaii and the whole extended family had gone. Emily would have liked to say they'd gone in the spirit of Aloha, but the truth was they'd all jumped at the free trip. They'd learned their lesson, though. No number of tropical sunsets or cocktails could make up for Helen's unpleasantness.

"I don't care if there are twenty-foot waves," surfer dude Connor texted Emily as their father's 73rd birthday loomed. "Never again. I was depressed for two months."

"How are the kids?" Emily asked him now. His two boys were almost the same age as Leo and Henry. "I'm sorry the cousins couldn't get together."

Connor stabbed at his rack of lamb. "Yeah, the boys do have a good time together. Too expensive now to bring us all down here."

Emily knew her father was paying for everyone's trip—Connor's excuse was so hollow it didn't come close to having a ring.

"Leo has started looking at colleges. We're hoping he can get a baseball scholarship. What about Edward? Is he thinking about schools yet?" she asked.

Connor shook his head. "Ed wants to be an outdoors guide—lead people on treks, river rafting—that sort of thing."

"Cool," Emily said, not meaning it at all. Education was so important to a person's future, she'd die if her sons didn't go to college. She'd kill herself if they wanted to aimlessly wander in nature for 40 years.

With her hypocritical response hanging in the air, Emily couldn't think of anything else to say to the brother she'd once been so close to. She and Connor had been a team, high functioning in their coordinated defense against their mother. They became so adept at their verbal volleys that the dinner hours had turned from Torquemada Time to Comedy Central. Momma dearest didn't do well with humor, so it became their deflecting tool. They'd helped each other survive, but now the tie was broken.

When Emily turned back toward Daniel, he was gone. His napkin sat atop his congealing sole meunière. Next to his plate was his iPhone.

How odd he'd left it there. She'd begun to think of it as an extension to Daniel's hands. She swore his thumbs twitched if he wasn't texting for a while.

As she stared at the phone it appeared to grow larger, even to glow. It called to her with the mega-strength of the ancient Sirens. For the first time, she had empathy for Odysseus. She felt the lure—felt the strongest urge to pick up the iPhone and read Daniel's messages. Then she thought of Tiger Woods' wife…what was her name? Ellen, Elin? Why had she been so compelled to look at Tiger's phone on a Thanksgiving night? Emily had been listening to the news on the radio when she heard about it. Sitting in her car at a stop light, Emily had thought it one of the saddest parts of that sordid story. On Thanksgiving night, you should be sitting around with your family, replete from the Pilgrimish feast, and counting your blessings. Instead, the Woods family imploded.

So learn from others, Emily told herself. Do not grab that phone and open a Pandora's box at Dad's birthday party.

Startled, Emily sat still for a moment, like a rabbit scenting the air for danger. Where had the Pandora thought come from? Why would looking at Daniel's messages stir up problems? She must subconsciously think Daniel was hiding something from her. Something she didn't want to know about—wouldn't be able to handle if she did.

She leaned away from the phone, from its temptation and the darkness it might contain. Then she told herself she was being ridiculous. She put a smile on her face and scanned the table. Her father was patting her mother's hand. Mother's mouth was pinched. Nothing new from that quarter. Dad spent most of his life trying to placate her royal highness. God, my poor dad, Emily thought, and sighed.

She looked down at her nearly full plate. She had been ravenous before the meal was served, but after a few bites—well, to be strictly honest, after Daniel's bitten-off rejection, she'd lost her appetite. Now her stomach hurt. She pushed away from the table.

"I'm going to the ladies'," she told Connor.

He gave her an eye roll. "Leaving the scene of the crime?"

She eye-rolled him back. "Don't you mean the impending train wreck? Sometimes retreat is the smartest strategy."

Connor laughed. Emily, delighted, pinched his cheek before she turned to weave her way between the tables toward the restroom. Her thoughts returned to Daniel. He'd been gone for at least 20 minutes.

Once in the hall, she could see a man standing outside the restaurant smoking. Well, that couldn't be Daniel. Daniel didn't smoke, she thought. But when the man straightened, she saw him more clearly. It was Daniel. What was going on?

She started toward the exit, but stopped. By the way Daniel held the cigarette, she realized he was smoking marijuana. "What the hell?"

She pushed the door open. "What the hell?" she repeated, much louder.

Daniel looked up and dropped the joint, grinding it under his foot. "What are you doing out here?" he asked.

"Me? What are you doing out here, besides smoking dope at my father's birthday party?"

"Aw, Jesus, here we go. Now you're going to make a big deal out of nothing."

"It's not a big deal? It's normal for you, smoking dope? You do it all the time?"

He held up his hand. "Stop screaming, okay? What are you doing out here? Spying on me?"

"Does marijuana make you paranoid? I'm not screaming and why would I be spying on you?" Emily shook her head. "I couldn't believe you left your iPhone on the table. But if you're smoking dope all the time, no wonder you're not working on all cylinders."

"What?" Daniel sounded panicked. He patted his blazer pocket. Finding it empty, he advanced on Emily. "Where is it? Did you touch it? Did you go through my messages?"

She backed up a few steps. "No, I didn't touch your precious phone, and I didn't look at your messages. The sorry truth is I was afraid what I'd find out about you. It made me realize I don't know you anymore."

Daniel worked his mouth like he was chewing on words he might say.

"I want to know what's going on, Daniel. I mean it."

The look he gave her was such a mixture of anger and bravado that she cringed. Whatever he had to say, it was going to be bad.

"Okay, Emily, you want to know what's going on? Here's the truth. I lost my fucking job."

"What?"

"Yeah, all those messages on my phone are from employment agencies," he said. "So now do you feel better? Now that you know I'm a fucking loser?"

He was shouting now. Emily blinked a few times as she tried to digest his words. Daniel, out of work. Daniel, not telling her. Daniel, so filled with rage.

"No quick quip, Em? That's not like you."

"I don't think you're a loser," she finally said, ignoring his taunt.

"Yeah, sure."

"I don't! Of course I don't. Why would I?" She took a deep breath. "But when did this happen?"

Daniel looked away. "About a month ago."

"You got fired a month ago? Why didn't you tell me?"

She shook her head. "I've always thought we were a team, Daniel. We're a family. You didn't have to go through this alone."

She put her hand out, but he pulled away.

"Get real, for once, Emily, instead of hiding in your little fantasy life where everything's always perfect."

Emily crossed her hands over her chest. "I'm not like that."

"Oh, yes you are. Or you think you can help make it okay," Daniel said with disdain. "If I'd told you, you'd be giving me a pep talk every morning that I'd be finding a job with no problem. But you know what? I'm almost fifty. Companies aren't interested in me. They're not going to hire me when they can get younger, sharper guys."

"But I know you. You're fantastic. You'll find another job."

"Shit, see what I mean? Always the little Pollyanna. You just don't get it."

He gave a harsh laugh and brushed past her.

"Where are you going?" she called after him.

He kept walking. "Back inside. Isn't it time for Daddy's birthday cake? You wouldn't want to miss that. Daddy is so special after all."

"That's not fair," she said. "You make it sound like I favor my dad over you. You're as important to me as he is. More important."

"Yeah, tell me another one."

She looked at his back, wondering at his bitterness. "Daniel, don't leave. We need to talk."

"Talk to yourself if you want to. I don't have anything more to say."

He pulled open the door and let it slam behind him.

The sound chilled Emily even more than the desert night air. She shivered and walked toward the restaurant. She'd never felt so shattered. Daniel losing his job was just a problem—it could be solved. What devastated her was that he hadn't trusted her enough to tell her. She had failed him big-time.

She went to the ladies' room and splashed cold water on her face. She looked up into the mirror, catching herself unawares. In the reflection, she saw she looked just like her father. It was the expression in the eyes—the same bleak resignation.

In the Corners of My Mind

I stuck my head out the door. Seeing nothing, I stood stock-still, listening for danger. There was only silence. I took a gulp of air, latched the door behind me, and shot across the apartment foyer. Only when I was outside, did I let out my breath. I was safe again.

My father told me my fears were silly. "It's only the radio," he said. "Old Mr. Swanson is hard of hearing so he turns up the volume, especially when President Eisenhower is talking."

In the entirety of my four-and-a-half years, Daddy had never been wrong. But he did have his limits—he was a grown up. He'd forgotten about the monsters and giants hiding everywhere. I knew about them and was sure I'd heard the words, "Fee, Fi, Fo, Fum" coming from above many times. Since I didn't want to worry my parents, I'd made this plan to get out of our apartment building without being captured and eaten. So far it had worked.

It was a rainy afternoon in Seattle, nothing unusual about that. My mother letting me go to Chi Chi's building by myself—now that was something new. Mother was expecting our baby, and she had a headache. So even though I'd be alone, she'd told me I could go.

Chi Chi was my best friend. As I walked along, (careful not to step on a crack so I wouldn't break my mother's back) I couldn't wait to tell her my plan. I'd wanted to explore the covered bus stop ever since my big brother showed me the yo-yo he'd found there.

"You took it?" I asked him.

"Sure," David said. "Finders keepers."

The bus stop was only a block from Chi Chi's, but it was outside of Edgewater, our apartment complex of ivy-covered buildings. We weren't allowed to leave Edgewater's perimeter but if Chi Chi were with me, I thought we could chance it. Who knew what we could find?

When I knocked on Chi Chi's door, nothing happened. I knocked again, but still no answer. It was dark in her foyer, so after a minute, I hurried outside.

In that short time, the rain had stopped. I decided to sit on the curb and wait. Ants hurried back and forth in the gutter as if they were late, late for a very important date. They marched in single file, one ant carrying a burden almost as big as she was.

A breeze blew the bangs away from my reddened forehead.

The summer before, my grandmother accidentally knocked a pot of coffee off the kitchen counter. I'd been standing next to her. The coffee shot down, scalding my forehead. I remember the coffee pot tilting, its chrome gleaming in the morning sunlight. But then I don't remember anything until I heard my grandmother's voice.

"What am I going to tell your mother," she wailed. Then, "*Gott, shreck mer, struff mer nisht.*" She repeated the Yiddish proverb: "Please God, frighten me, don't strike me." As my grandmother rocked back and forth, I tried opening my eyes, but they felt glued together.

I stirred in the nest of blankets I was wrapped in.

At my movement, Bubbe Esther whispered, "Thanks, Gott." She continued rocking, humming at first and then singing a lullaby. She stopped only when my grandfather came pounding up the porch steps. That's when I realized we were on the screened-in-porch at the front of their house.

What I didn't know, as I lay cradled in the warmth of my grandmother, was that my cousin had been hit by a car and killed in Seaside, Oregon a few months before. He'd run into the street after a ball our older cousin had thrown.

Rocky was my age. I didn't even know of his existence until I was 33.

My husband and I had planned a trip to Seaside with our two children. My mother went nuts when I told her.

"You can't go there," she'd said.

I was totally exasperated with her meddling. "That's ridiculous. We're going."

"It's a dangerous place."

I rolled my eyes. "It's a little honky tonk, but it's just a seaside resort."

"People die there," she said.

"Mother, you're exaggerating again."

And that's when she told me what had happened thirty years before. How my grandparents, aunts and cousins had been standing on the sidewalk. How the car appeared out of nowhere. How no one could stop Rocky from going after the ball. How each blamed themselves.

No wonder my grandfather's hand shook that day as he placed it on top of my head. No wonder my grandmother rocked me as if she were in a trance. They probably felt they were in the midst of an unending nightmare. Would another grandchild be taken from them?

"I brought the doctor," my grandfather said.

"Thanks, Gott." Then, hesitant, she asked, "Doctor, will she be all right?"

"Let me see the child before you ask me questions like that," the doctor said.

I remember the feel of his cool hand on my forehead. Smooth, unlike my grandfather's, it burned as if I were being scalded again.

"Let's get some butter on this right away," the doctor ordered. "And we need some cold towels."

The front door banged as my grandfather hurried into the house.

"Now, girl, sit still in your grandmother's lap so I can check your eyes," the doctor ordered.

My grandmother gripped me tightly. "Oh, please Gott, don't let her be blind."

The doctor prodded at my eyes, forcing them open. It felt like the Sandman had left his whole load in them. But after blinking several minutes, things cleared. I looked into the doctor's stern face with the round glasses, and the gray moustache with scrambled egg on it.

And that's all I remember of that morning. While some details etched themselves into my memory, the rest is gone. I know my mother had my hair cut with bangs to hide the blistered skin, and fussed that I would be scarred for life. But that's all.

Eight months later I stood in front of Chi Chi's willing her to come home, not giving my forehead another thought.

When I felt a drop of rain on my head, I looked up at a sky heavy with clouds. I wondered if I should go back. Would Mother want me there? I got up and started in the direction of home.

Then I thought, it's so close. I can get to it and back in no time.

I turned and made a beeline for the bus stop. I pictured myself looking under the wooden bench as raindrops pinged against the tin roof. What treasure would I find?

But then I stopped. What if the Boogey Man was there? "Little girl. You want some candy?" he might ask and grab me.

I turned fast and sprinted past Chi Chi's, following the circle to our building. I was soaked by the time I made it into our foyer. This time I heard the giant's footsteps stomping on the floorboards upstairs.

I ran to our door and opened it. Mother was standing in the entry, wringing her hands. Her worried frown turned to relief as she saw me.

"Thank God, you're safe. I should never have let you go out alone," she said.

She pulled me close—I could feel her shaking.

"It's not safe out there," she whispered into my hair. "It's not safe."

I believed her for years.

JUST ONCE

Let's get something straight from the get-go. I hate bullshit and I hate bullshitters. Don't ask me for nicey-nice—you're not going to get it. So how the hell did I get myself into this situation?

I guess this is what happens when I try to be a good guy. You see, Brenda was in so much fucking trouble. Ralph was just trying to help her, and I figured he needed my support.

I met Brenda through Marty and Ralph. We're all from Highland Park, outside Chicago, and go to Palm Springs every winter. None of our wives play golf, but we're addicted. One day I'd just parred the tenth hole when I leaned over to pick up the ball and that was it. I couldn't straighten up.

"No problem," Ralph said. "I got a great massage therapist. As soon as we finish the round, I'll take you over there."

"What the hell am I supposed to do while you play eight more holes?" I asked. "I'm going home."

Ralph gave me the look. He was a retired CEO and had developed this killer stare. I hate to admit it, but it even works on me.

Eight holes later they pushed me into the back seat of his Cadillac SUV. He'd already called the massage therapist from the course, but he called her again. It didn't occur to me until much later to wonder why he had her on speed dial.

Brenda lived in this trailer court just off Monterrey in Palm Desert. Her trailer was small, but okay. It was like going back to the '70s when you walked in the door. There was some incense burning by a poster of a guru-looking guy, but you could still smell the marijuana. And I remember thinking I could smell alcohol on her breath too. Whatever, she did give a great massage. She got real deep into the tissues. By the end of the hour, I could stand straight, and it only hurt a little.

So I started going to Brenda once a week for a massage. In no time my back was the best it had been for years. I knew Marty went once a week too, but Ralph went three times a week. He'd made it big with Apple stock and could afford it.

In February, after our regular Wednesday game, we were eating lunch and started talking about the coming summer.

"You know, I've been thinking," Ralph said. "Why don't we bring Brenda to Chicago when we go back home?"

I had just taken a huge bite of my pastrami sandwich and almost choked on it. "What the hell for?" I asked.

"Well, she's the best massage therapist I ever had. And she told me she wanted to get out of Palm Springs in the summer. The heat is killing her."

"Where would she live?" Marty asked. He sounded real skeptical, just like I felt.

"We could find her one of those small furnished apartments and help her out with the rent until she gets some clients and can manage on her own."

"Are you kidding me! Help her out? I've got two kids and five grandchildren I'm helping out. I can't afford to help anyone else out," I said.

"Then I'll pay for it," Ralph said. Real casual like, he took a cigar out of his case and snipped off the end.

I shoulda known then and there to back away, but did I? No, not me. I just finished my sandwich and said yes to the waitress on a refill of my Diet Coke. I was a yes man that day and look where it got me.

So Brenda came to Chicago at the end of May. Ralph had found her a furnished studio apartment near Highland Park. I didn't think much one way or another about her being there—my priority was worrying about my golf game and the Cubs. But I did feel a little uneasy that we decided not to tell our wives.

"They'll just make something out of nothing," Ralph said. Not liking it, I still went along with him.

It was on my second visit to Brenda that it began to get complicated. When she let me in, she looked like hell. The apartment didn't look much better. It wasn't just that it was dingy and dark. It was a mess. The cheap rental furniture was covered with all kinds of shit. Her trailer had always been neat and tidy.

Once I was on the massage table, I closed my eyes and tried to relax. I was there for a massage, I told myself. Her problems were not my problems. Usually she played some hippy-dippy kind of music on Pandora, but that day she didn't.

"I just need someone I can talk to," she said.

Uh-oh, I thought. Famous last words.

But what was I supposed to do? She had me captive on the table. By the time she finished the massage, she'd told me how she'd been abused by her father and her ex-husband. She was also slurring her words big time.

"But I really wanted to talk to you about Ralph," she said when I was paying her. She liked cash and I liked paying with it—no trail.

"I gotta go," I said. I tossed an extra ten bucks on the table and got the hell out of there.

By July I was trying to get out of my appointments. She was shit-faced no matter how early it was. And she wanted to talk the whole time. I began to miss the creepy music on her iPhone. Like I said before, I'm not a touchy-feely kinda guy. The best massage in the world wasn't worth listening to her crap.

When she started to talk about Ralph, I put the kibosh on that immediately. No way, José, I wasn't going there.

"You want to tell me about your kid who went to live with your cocaine-addict ex-husband, fine. But Ralph is off limits," I said.

As the weeks went by, she'd try to get Ralph back into the conversation, but I'd stop her. Once she started crying so hard she had to quit the massage. I'll tell you I was a little pissed, but what could I do? I ended up with my arm around her shoulder, trying to get her to calm down. I wanted to get my damn massage, didn't I? She kept saying her life was ruined and she had no future.

"No, it isn't," I said, but the truth? Her life was in the toilet. And if she'd been counting on Ralph to be her knight in shining armor, she was totally delusional.

Warning bells were ringing in both my ears that day, or the stress was making my tinnitus much worse. Whatever, I knew things were getting out of hand. I just didn't know how much.

It had been raining that week so we had to cancel golf, but Ralph called and said we needed to talk.

Jesus Christ, I thought. What now?

We met at the Starbucks in Winnetka. Ralph had a Frappuccino and I had an Americano. I'm pre-diabetic so I gotta watch my sugar.

I took a sip of my coffee. "So what's up?"

"I'm worried about Brenda," Ralph said.

No shit, Sherlock, I thought. "Worried about what?" I said.

He looked at me. "This is between the two of us. We're not even telling Marty any of it." Marty and his wife, Donna, were on a four-week cruise in Europe. I'd thought he was such a sucker to get talked into it, but now he seemed like the winner.

"Okay. It's just between you and me. What is it?"

I was pretty sure he was going to tell me he was schtuping Brenda. I didn't want to hear it. That would make me an accessory after the fact, but the options were closing down. "Tell me already," I said.

"Well, you know I have been getting closer and closer to Brenda. She's a nice woman."

"Yeah, okay. So why the need for a powwow?"

Ralph cleared his throat like he was real nervous. "I'm pretty sure she's an alcoholic. You must have noticed that she's always drinking."

I nodded. I felt so relieved this was what was going to be the topic— I didn't want to be Father Confessor.

"So, I talked to her about rehab. I found a place for her to go. They can take her in three weeks."

"Jesus," I said. At the same time I felt my phone vibrate against my thigh.

I pulled it out of my pocket and checked the Caller ID. "It's Brenda. She's been calling me two-three times a day."

"Yeah, me too," Ralph said. He twisted the ring on his little finger.

"It's driving me crazy," I said. "And she's always drunk."

"I know. That's why I'm setting her up for rehab."

Ralph outlined his plan and how he wanted my help. I wasn't crazy about it, but I agreed.

So now it's three weeks later and you're just about current. Brenda was all set to go into rehab tomorrow. Ralph and I were picking her up in the morning and driving her to a place in Wisconsin. She started calling me at ten this morning. I was sick and tired of her calls and I was playing golf.

What the hell, I said to myself. She can wait until I'm done.

When I called her back after lunch, there was no answer. I didn't think much about it until Judge Judy was over. I called Brenda again and didn't get an answer.

At about 7:00 I called Ralph.

"You talk to Brenda today?" I asked.

"Yeah, early. I've been gone all day. You know our grandson, Taylor. It's his tenth birthday so went to Wrigley." He paused. "Why do you want to know if I talked to Brenda?"

"Well, she called me a bunch of times, but when I called her back this afternoon, she never picked up. I just called her again and there was no answer. Was she going anyplace?"

"I don't think so. She said she was getting ready to leave tomorrow. Let me give her a call right now."

Fifteen minutes later he called me back. "No answer. I think I'm going to go over to her place. Will you come?"

It was the last thing I wanted to do, but I couldn't see how to get out of it. I was beginning to feel very guilty—I could have texted Brenda back at least once.

I gave my wife some sort of excuse and was standing outside when Ralph drove up. We made the trip to Brenda's in silence. I was beginning to picture all kinds of things, one worse than the other.

Her front door had one of those knockers and Ralph used it. He waited a minute and hit it again, louder. After he did this a couple more times, he pulled out his key chain.

He had a fuckin' key? I couldn't believe it.

He opened the door and called, "Brenda?"

When there was no answer, we walked into the apartment. The living room was totally trashed. The massage table was turned on its side, clothes were thrown everywhere, and a lamp was smashed. It looked like someone had thrown it against the wall. Three or four empty bottles of booze were next to the couch.

Ralph and I looked at each other.

"Fuck," he said. "What the hell happened in here?"

He pushed his way around the mess until he was in the hall. I was still by the door.

He turned to look at me. "Are you coming?"

I don't remember if I said anything, but I did follow him. By then I was sweating—I don't know if it was because the place was hotter than hell or if it was because I was so fucking scared of what we were going to find. I started imagining she'd cut her wrists or something.

"Brenda?" Ralph called out.

There wasn't much of a hallway—the place was so small. When we got to the bedroom, the door was closed.

Ralph knocked. "Brenda?"

When there was no answer, he opened the door. She wasn't in the bedroom either. I began to hope all my worst fears were just too many CSI shows, and she was out shopping or something. Maybe for cleaning supplies. But then I saw a light coming from under the bathroom door.

"She could be in the bathroom and didn't hear us," I said.

"Let's hope."

Ralph pushed open the door. She was there all right, but everything was wrong. She was in the tub with her head half under the water.

"Oh my God!" Ralph said. "Shit!"

He ran across the room, kicking liquor bottles out of his way.

"Call 911," he yelled.

My hands were shaking so much I had trouble getting my phone out. I punched in the numbers as I watched him grab the back of Brenda's head and yank her face out of the water.

I told the emergency operator what had happened and where we were. He started asking me questions, but Ralph was yelling for help so I just dropped my phone and rushed over to him.

"Come on, Brenda," he said. "Come on." He slapped her cheeks like that could wake her up, but I knew it was too late. Her lips were already blue. I'd been in Vietnam and seen several dead bodies.

"She's not breathing," Ralph said. "We have to get her out of the tub so we can do CPR."

I wanted to say, "She's dead," but he was close to hysterical so I kept quiet.

We managed to get her out, but it was difficult. Her whole body seemed waterlogged. And she kept slipping out of our hands. Ralph tried CPR to get her breathing. Then I tried. It was gross, but we were still trying when the paramedics came and took over.

Now we're sitting in the police station in different interrogation rooms. They keep asking me the same questions over and over. Did she take pills? Was she suicidal? Had I been there that morning? What time did we get there?

I keep telling them what happened. But really all I can think of is Brenda's bloated face. I know I'll never forget it. And I do keep asking myself one question: What if I had answered just one of her phone calls? Just once.

KHRUSHCHEV IN MY DREAMS

I lay in bed, trying to fall asleep, but I was too afraid. There was a pretty good chance I'd be dead within the month—me and the rest of the world.

"Carol, don't be so dramatic," my dad said the next morning at breakfast. "You're worrying for nothing. Mother and I have lived through a lot worse threats. The Russians are just playing chicken with us."

Fine for him to say, I thought. He's old—fifty-three. He'd already lived his life. I was fifteen and hadn't lived at all. I'd never even had a boyfriend. If the Russians didn't turn back their ships, there would be nuclear war.

I sat at the table, gagging down the glass of milk my mother insisted I have every morning even though I told her it gave me a stomachache. My parents never listened to me. They told me they knew best. And it was typical of my dad to make light of my fears. They were the children of immigrants who had fled pogroms. My grandmother had almost been killed by Cossacks.

"Those were real problems," Mother said as if the threat of nuclear winter was nothing.

They didn't know the terror that lived within me—that wouldn't let me rest. My fears had started when I very young—during the Korean War. I was scared to death that we'd need to use the bomb shelter Mother created in the basement under the stairs.

"What if a bomb falls from the sky toward our house?" I asked my brother back then. I could see a cartoon bowling-ball bomb with its firecracker fuse hurtling across the lake, zeroing in on our street.

Steve, who always protected me, said, "If they throw a bomb at us, I'll catch it and throw it back."

I believed he could do it and was comforted enough that I stopped biting my nails to the quick. Eventually events evened out—the bomb shelter became a playhouse where we enacted stories of survival. We used the Sterno cans still stored there to cook cocktail hotdogs I'd pilfer from the fridge.

Life moved on and teenage angst superseded fears of annihilation. That is, until the fall of 1962. The Russians were building nuclear reactors in Cuba, refusing American demands that they cease and desist. With all the saber rattling, it felt as if Armageddon was at hand. I was a complete wreck. Even when I did fall asleep, I'd have dreams of Khrushchev pounding his shoe on our dining room table.

My friends and I believed the end of the planet was inevitable. We'd all seen the movie, *On the Beach*, which fed our fears. It prophesized that World War III would culminate in nuclear war in 1963, causing the immediate destruction of the northern hemisphere. Let me tell you, it was nightmare-producing.

So on October 28, 1962, despite my parents' assurances that all would be well, we were sure it was the beginning of the end. Soviet ships were within sight of the Americans—we knew that it was a matter of hours before the clash could begin.

I was editor of the high-school newspaper that semester. That morning, three junior editors and I were working on putting the newspaper to bed. Full of trepidation, we were unable to concentrate. Instead, we hunkered around the transistor radio on my desk, thirsty for news of the U.S./Soviet confrontation. (Our advisor was off somewhere drinking coffee, or perhaps it was whiskey, so we had free rein to do whatever we wished.)

When regularly scheduled broadcasting was interrupted for a news flash, we all looked at each other with trepidation.

"What do you think this means?" Tomoko asked.

"It can't be good," Bill said.

We all leaned closer to the little radio as if it would answer our deepest fears.

"It has been confirmed," the announcer said. "The Soviet ships are turning around to return to the Soviet Union. Khrushchev has announced that the missile sites in Cuba will be dismantled." He was almost shouting at the end, his voice jubilant with relief.

The four of us looked at each other. We weren't close friends at all—just joined by our mutual interest in the newspaper. But we simultaneously reached out and hugged each other.

"I'm going to go tell the principal," I said. "He'll announce it to the school."

I ran down the steps to the office, sure that Mr. Hanawalt would be thrilled with the news and would want to allay the fears of all the students.

"I need to see Mr. Hanawalt," I told the school secretary.

"Do you have a hall pass, Carol Ann?" she asked.

"No, but this is important. The Russians have turned back!" I said.

She gave me an odd look, but buzzed to let him know I was there. I didn't have to wait long.

Mr. Hanawalt was sitting at his desk when I burst into his office.

I explained to him what we'd just heard. "The Russians have turned back! You have to let everyone know," I said. "Announce it on the PA system."

He looked at me consideringly, then shook his head. "No, that wouldn't be a good idea."

"Why?" I couldn't believe he was refusing.

He sat back in his chair, amusement brimming in his eyes. He was a medium-sized man who wore rumpled nondescript suits. He always seemed calm, which had to be a challenge in a school like Garfield. (Forget marijuana; heroin was the main drug of choice for those so inclined. Knife fights were common on certain stairways, as I'd learned from an unfortunate experience the day I came close to walking within inches of Carl's switchblade. I'd known Carl since first grade and he'd waved me back with a "Carol Ann, get out of here," warning.)

Mr. Hanawalt ran his hand over the bristles of his crew cut. "Don't you worry about it—just go back to class. I'll handle it," he said.

I rolled my eyes, turned, and went back to the newspaper office.

"He won't do it," I said when I came in.

"Why not?" Tomoko asked. She, like many of my Japanese friends, had been born in Hunt, Idaho. Which I always thought was a little strange. And they never talked about it.

I shook my head. "I don't know. You'd think he'd want to let everyone know we'll be okay. I just don't get people sometimes."

"I guess this means we've got to get back to work on this edition," Bill joked.

So after we walked across the street and bought hamburgers and milkshakes, we did.

Nuclear war had been averted. We could breathe again.

Late Bloomer

I hate first dates. Man, are they awful! Not that I've had so many—just one, to be exact.

Hey, I'm only 16. I'm new at this girl thing. And my first date with Carly was such a disaster, I almost swore off dating forever, right then and there.

I asked Carly out because—well, because Keith, my buddy, forced me into it. He told me she liked me. I thought that was cool because she is hot. So I kept looking at her. Then I caught her looking at me.

At lunch one day, Keith told me he couldn't stand all the looks going back and forth.

"Dude, call and ask her out. Don't be such a nerd," is what he really said.

So I decided I would. It wasn't like we were strangers. She was in my fifth period Chemistry class. Besides, I'd known her since we were in kindergarten.

But after I dialed her number, I got throat-lock. My mind went blank like I had amnesia of words. Me and my friends play a lot of sports—we're not into talking. But even I'm smart enough to have known this was different. I shoulda planned something.

I was about to hang up when someone at the other end said, "Hello."

"Ah, ah, hello. Is, is Carly there?" *I was going to start stuttering, now?*

"This is Carly."

Right there I got stuck again. Finally I said, "Oh." That's right, I said, "Oh," and nothing else.

Carly must have thought it was a weirdo calling. "Who IS this?" she asked, real suspicious-like.

Her tone jump-started my brain. "Ah, hi, it's Bradley."

"Bradley? Bradley who?"

Now, come on. How many Bradleys are there in this world? And didn't she have Caller ID? She had to know it was me, but I played along. "Bradley Vernon. You know. In fifth period, Mr. Kiemle's class."

"Oh, that Bradley."

"Yeah. Uh, would you like to go out on Saturday night?" *Hey, why waste time? Get the question out like a good fast ball.*

"You mean tomorrow night?"

"Yeah."

"Oh, I'm sorry, but I have to baby-sit."

Why do girls baby-sit? I wondered. "How 'bout tomorrow afternoon?"

"Can't. I go skiing."

"How about Sunday?" I wanted to lock in a date so I didn't waste a phone call.

"Sorry, but I have to do homework."

Carly did sound apologetic. . . not very, but some. Still, I was getting discouraged. "Well, 'bye," I said.

Head hanging, I climbed the stairs to my parents' bedroom. They were getting ready to go out to some dinner for my dad's office so I knocked on their door. "Hey, you guys decent?"

Dad opened the door. "Depends on your definition. Your mother is in the bathroom taking her usual hour and a half to get dressed. Come on in."

He started to cough. He was just getting over the flu.

I flopped down on their bed. "Well, I asked her."

"What did she say?" Mom's voice sounded squeezed tight. That meant she was putting on her mascara and didn't want to move her face.

"No."

Dad looked up from tying his shoe. "No? No, what?"

I sighed. "She said she had to baby-sit."

"You should have asked her sooner," Dad said like he was an authority on dating. What could he know? He hadn't had a date since before Russia was a part of the Soviet Union.

I was about to point this out to him, when the telephone rang. I leaned over and picked it up from the bedside table. "Hello."

"Hi, Bradley? This is Carly. I got someone else to baby-sit for me tomorrow night so I can go."

"Really? Cool. Okay. I'll pick you up at eight. 'Bye."

I put the phone back and jumped off the bed. "Yesssss!" I punched the air like I just won the U.S. Open.

Mom came into the room, and squinted at me. Either she'd decided not to wear her contacts or she couldn't believe what she was seeing—her little boy growing up. "That had to be the shortest phone call in the history of peoplekind," she said.

"Short, but sweet, that's my motto." I saluted my parents and jogged out of the room.

The next night when I went to pick up Carly, I was a little early. I pulled to the curb in front of her house. I kept the engine running so I could listen to Cold Play on the radio. My hair does this thing—it just sort of flops over. I was sticking my fingers through it—wishing I'd used more gel, and sorta practicing my smile in the rear-view mirror—when I felt someone watching me. I looked over and saw Carly, standing by the car door. I hadn't heard her because the music was so loud.

My smile tightened like it had been shrink wrapped. I pressed the button to lower the window. "Oh, hi. Ready to go?"

"Uh huh." She opened the door and got in.

"Great." *Wonderful. I couldn't even come up with a full sentence.*

I couldn't think of anything more to say on the way to pick up Keith and his girlfriend, Shelly. Thankfully, Carly asked me what movie we were going to see.

" *'Night Terror*," I said.

"Oh, cool! I never got to see that and I've been dying to."

"Great, 'cuz there's lots of dying in it."

Carly laughed. *Hey, things were looking up!*

I felt pretty good by the time we were at the theater. The four of us were laughing and talking as we walked up to the box office.

"Four for *Night Terror*," I said like I did this every day.

"*Night Terror*? That ain't been playing here for months, buddy," the jerk behind the glass said.

I looked at the others. "Sorry, I guess we'll have to decide on another movie."

The next film didn't start for forty-five minutes, so we went to play the video machines. I got to concentrating real hard playing RoboRoller. I leaned in close and POW, knocked my head into it. That machine started shrieking like a car alarm. Finally, a guy came over and turned a key to stop the noise.

After he left, Carly handed me her coke. "It's got ice in it. Put it on that bump on your forehead."

Wasn't that smart, not to mention cool? I could see she was starting to care.

Once we were seated, and the lights dimmed, things got a little confusing. Keith and Shelly started holding hands. It made me nervous. Should I hold Carly's hand? Would she think I was making a move on her if I did? Would she think I was a nerd if I didn't? Like I said, I was new to the dating game so what did I know? I was so worried, I couldn't pay attention to the movie and it had cost me 18 bucks.

Afterwards, Keith and Shelly wanted to go get something to eat. I wasn't very hungry—I had a terrible headache. At the restaurant, we had to wait for about a half an hour. When the girls went to the bathroom, Keith started dissing me.

"Dude, I can't believe you. You didn't even try to hold her hand."

"How would you know? You seemed awfully involved with Shelly to be watching what I was doing."

"Some of us can do two things at once. Why didn't you even try?"

"It's our first date!"

Keith made a snorting-gagging sound. "Dude, you are so uncool."

"Yeah? Well, I'll just ask that blond lady over there what she thinks."

I walked over to the hostess desk. "Pardon me. May I ask you a personal question?"

The woman was old, at least 25. The look she gave me could have frozen hot soup. "Listen, kid. My boyfriend is 6'5", so you'd better watch it."

"I'm not here to start trouble. I just wanted you to ask you something. My friend says I shoulda held Carly's hand in the movie, but I said no way. It was our first date. What do you think?"

"You're worried about holding a girl's hand? What a wuss!"

I gave the old bag a dirty look and turned around. There were the girls, listening to every word. I closed my eyes. *Could I just be beamed up to some far away planet?*

I could feel my face getting red. When that happens, my freckles blend into a solid tomato mass. What with the lump on my forehead, I wasn't a pretty picture.

Finally we were seated. I was so relieved I leaned back into the plastic upholstery of the booth. That turned out to be a problem, too. I leaned back so hard, I knocked the water pitcher off the table behind us. Do you know how far shattered glass travels?

You probably think I made all this up, but I didn't. Just ask Carly, she'll tell you. We've been a couple for four months, now.

We talked about it just last week in the waiting room at the Cancer Center. Me and Carly take my dad there for his chemo appointments. It turned out his cough wasn't from the flu, after all. It was lung cancer, but he's going to be all right after the chemo and stuff. That's what my mom told us.

Anyway, Carly says I was kind of weird when we first went out, but since she's known me since kindergarten, she decided to chalk it up to first date jitters.

I told you she was cool.

MID-SOLSTICE NIGHT DREAMING

Summer was knocking on the door of June that evening we got together for a quick dinner. Although it was almost seven, the sun still shone high above the horizon as we entered the restaurant. Holding my right hand was Garrett, my four-year-old grandson. Squeezing my left was Evan, the three-year-old.

"Welcome to Pizza Magic. You guys want a table for three?" The girl at the hostess desk sounded irritated—as if our coming in the door had interrupted her from doing something important.

"No, there'll be six of us. One booster seat, please," I said, trying not to stare at the ring looped between the girl's nostrils. It didn't look clean, which was something I'd rather not know about. If this was how the hostess presented herself to the public, what about the cook hidden away in the kitchen? I began to picture a guy with long hair as greasy as his apron, twirling pizza dough with bacteria-coated fingers.

Evan tugged on my hand. "I don't want a booster seat, Grammy."

"It's not for you—it's for cousin Eli. He's meeting us with his mommy."

I leaned down to retie my running shoe, counting to ten. Had I sounded annoyed? I hoped not. I usually was so calm with the boys, much more than I'd been with my own children. But Garrett and Evan had stayed over last night, and for the first time they hadn't listened to a word I said. They wouldn't brush their teeth or settle down after I'd read them stories. I'd had to resort to time-outs for both of them.

Of course, I understood why they were so unruly. There'd been a lot going on in the family these last few months—with today being the topper.

"Marianne, are they going to seat us or should we go somewhere else?"

I looked up. My husband, lines of fatigue around his eyes, loomed over me. I crossed my fingers, hoping he'd have enough patience to get through the next few hours. Patience was his short suit.

"Robert, calm down. The girl said it would be about five minutes for a table. Lisa and Eli aren't here yet, anyway."

Garrett took Robert's hand. "Daddo, will you take us to see the fountain?"

Robert sighed. "All right, but just for a minute. Come on, Evan. You come, too." He held out his hand. Evan deposited the tattered remnants of his baby blanket into it.

"I'm going to give your blankie to Grammy. She'll take care of it." Robert tossed the blanket to me. Evan's eyes followed its flight as if it were a World Series strike out pitch in the bottom of the ninth.

"Come on, guys. Let's go throw some pennies in the fountain and make a wish." Robert had his arms around both boys as they walked out the door.

I sat down on a bench near the restaurant's entrance and closed my eyes. It felt good to just rest for a moment. If anyone had told me I'd have four grandchildren by the time I was 53, I wouldn't have believed them. I always thought grandparents were old. I didn't feel old—present time excepted.

"There's Grammy, Eli. I told you she'd be here."

I opened my eyes to see my daughter and third grandson coming in the entrance. I held out my arms to Eli. "Come here, sweetie. Grammy missed you today."

Eli toddled over to me. I picked him up. "How was school? Did you have fun?"

He nodded, pleating the knitted blue and yellow blanket he held. I hugged him close. He wasn't even two yet. It broke my heart that he had to be in day-care from seven in the morning to six at night.

Lisa sank down next to me. "Oh, my feet," she moaned. She slipped off her high heels, and we both stared at the reddened blisters on her toes.

"How was work? Besides the fact that wearing those gorgeous shoes is killing your feet." I tried for an upbeat, teasing tone.

"It was okay. I mean it's only the second day. I was on the phone and the computer most of the time . . . you know, getting in contact with the client base."

Eli put his head on my shoulder and his thumb in his mouth. I looked at Lisa. She was brushing tears from her eyes. "What's the matter, honey?"

My question was almost rhetorical. I'd been asking it on a daily basis for more than a year. That her marriage hadn't worked out had devastated her and us, to be honest. Greg had seemed such a sensible person, but after 9-11, he'd decided he had to go his own way to find himself.

"I wanted to be a stay-at-home mom," Lisa said. "I just hate being away from Eli."

"Why do you hate being away from Eli?" Garrett asked.

Robert had returned with the boys. He bent down to kiss Eli and then Lisa.

"How was work?" he asked.

"Fine. I just miss being with Eli."

"Why do you miss being with Eli? Why isn't Uncle G having dinner with us?"

Garrett was in the why and why asking stage. If the sun was out, he wanted to know why. If the sun was setting, he wanted to know why. "Why did those men crash the airplanes into the buildings?" he'd asked me last September. "Why is our president, Mr. George W. Bush, an American, talking to us all the time on the radio and tv?"

I'd wanted to ask why a child, not even four years old, had to be burdened by these questions. Garrett also asked about Gregory's absence a lot. He'd even asked when Auntie Lisa and Uncle G were going to make up.

"I have to leave Eli because I have to work, sweetie," Lisa said. Her voice had become that of the attentive auntie, masking her own distress.

"But why?" Garrett asked again.

"Your table's ready." It was our gracious and lovely hostess, come to seat us. Thank God for small favors.

Fifteen minutes later, we had ordered. I'd let the boys get brown Sprite, as we called Coke just between ourselves, and they were happy drinking their forbidden treat. Eli watched them, grinning around his thumb and blanket.

"So, Garrett and Evan, are you guys excited about your new baby sister?" Lisa asked.

"Yeah, but we wants to see her," Evan said.

"I bet! I want to see her, too. Maybe Grammy will pick up Eli from daycare tomorrow? Then I can go visit at the hospital on my way home from work." Lisa turned to me.

I nodded assent. What else could I do? Even if I felt I was holding on by a fraying thread, I couldn't refuse. I had to help her out. But I was so tired—tired to the bone. Tired of all the sadness, tired of all the trauma—the struggles into life and out of it. It all seemed too much.

At least Quinn was perfectly healthy, even if the doctor had been worried she could be still born. He'd insisted on inducing my daughter-in-law three weeks early. Instead of a July baby, we had a June girl. A little redhead.

I should be feeling elated, I told myself. After all, Quinn had been born just four hours earlier.

I sat up straight. "Oh my goodness. It's Quinn's birth day—her real and only birth day. We have to sing "Happy Birth Day" to her right now!"

Lisa looked up from handing crayons out to the boys. "You're right, Mom. We need to sing."

"Marianne, you are so nuts," Robert said, his tone dismissive.

I turned my back on him. He thought I was nuts? Well, I thought he could teach the Grinch a lesson or two.

"Ready guys to sing? Garrett and Evan? Ready to sing for your new baby sister?" Lisa asked. I was grateful she was willing to enter into the spirit of things.

Garrett nodded his white-blond head. "Do you think she'll hear us?"

"I'm sure she will." I smiled at him. "Okay, all together now, one, two, three. Happy Birthday to Quinn," I began.

Robert rolled his eyes, but joined in. After we finished singing, I looked around the table. Each of us was smiling. It might have been a dorky thing to do, but it felt just fine . . . even better than fine.

"I wants my momma." Evan's plaintive drawl broke the spell.

Robert leaned towards me and whispered, "Where did Evan get his southern accent?"

I smiled, instantly in rapport with my husband once again. "I don't know, but his drawl gets thicker every day."

"Remember, Evan, Mommy is at the hospital with baby Quinn," Lisa said.

"But I wants my momma, now," Evan repeated.

I reached over to his plate. "You'll get to see her tomorrow, sweetie. Here, let me cut up your pizza for you."

"Grammy, Grammy. I want to ask you something." Garrett tugged at my sleeve.

"Not now, honey. I'm cutting up Evan's pizza."

"But it's important. It's about Grandpa Sid."

Grandpa Sid. My father who had died three weeks earlier. My beloved father.

Earlier in the birthing room, when I stood next to the doctor and watched Quinn's head emerge from my daughter-in-law's womb, it reminded me of the evening Dad had died. It felt like the same process, only in reverse. I'd been by Dad's bed, holding his hand all day long. I'd supported Dad on his final journey out of this life just as I helped Quinn on her journey into it.

I turned to Garrett. "Okay, honey, what do you want to know?"

"Is that what happens?"

"What, sweetie?"

"So when you die you go back to where it all began and then you start over again?"

I swallowed hard, startled by his succinct description. He spoke as if he had figured out the answer to a difficult equation.

I felt Lisa's hand seek out mine. I felt Robert's hand settle on my shoulder.

"That's a very smart idea. A lot of people think it happens just that way," I told Garrett when I could finally speak.

He smiled and his small shoulders relaxed. He picked up his slice of pizza and began to eat.

Later that night I dreamed that my father and Quinn were lying on individual sofas in a tunnel. The sofas were hooked together like train cars. Dad's train was faced in one direction, Quinn's in the other. But for three weeks, they sat side by side, and got to know each other very well.

MY FATHER'S STORY

Rain pelted Sidney's jacket, seeping under his collar as he hurried down the cobbled street. The clang of the trolley warned him to move to the inside of the boardwalk. Still, his pants were sprayed with rain and slush as the vehicle passed. His eyes followed its journey down the rails in the middle of the street. One day, he vowed, he'd have enough money to ride the trolley.

"No," he said aloud. "One day I won't need to ride the trolley. I'll drive myself around in my own car."

He straightened his thin shoulders and continued on his way. The further he went, the shabbier the surroundings became. Buildings in need of paint with half their windows broken, lined these roads. Holly Street, where his father had his clothing store, bordered Old Town, one of the roughest areas in Bellingham.

As Sidney turned the corner, he saw his father standing in front of his store. Papa had asked him to come by after school. All day, Sidney had wondered why. What did he want to say that couldn't be said at home? He knew by his father's agitated pacing that it had to be something important.

"Sidneyla," Papa called as Sidney hurried towards him. Papa put his arm around Sidney's shoulders, drawing him into the store.

"Oh, you're all wet. Come over by the stove," Papa said.

Sidney, shivering, followed his father.

"Your hands! Your hands! They are red with the cold." His father made a tsking sound. "Where are your gloves? Oy, your mother would kill you if she saw your hands. A concert pianist must always protect his hands."

Sidney shrugged. His gloves were too small so he'd given them to his little brother. Sollie could use them and Sidney could get along without. It was February and the weather would be getting warmer soon. As for being a concert pianist? His mother's dream, not his. He played all right, but he realized he didn't have what it took to be great. He wasn't a little boy anymore who believed everything his parents told him. Besides, he knew the future he wanted. He would go into business and make a fortune.

As he held his hands to the meager heat generated from the potbellied stove, he looked around Papa's store. Stacks of Levi jeans and bundles of flannel work shirts lay helter-skelter on wooden countertops. Papa hadn't even unpacked them for display. The cash register, with its elaborate metal curlicues that had cost so much, sat under a mantle of dust.

My business, Sidney vowed, will never look like this. I'll polish my business until it shines.

"Here, drink a little of this schnapps. It'll warm you up inside out."

Papa, holding out a small tumbler of golden liquid, brought Sidney back from the future.

"Papa. Whiskey? I can't drink that. It's illegal."

Papa shook his head. "Illegal-sh'megal. You're afraid of a little whiskey around? Who cares? Prohibition is the least of my problems."

A part of Sidney wondered what problems Papa had, but most of him was afraid to know.

"Where did you get the whiskey?" he asked to keep the topic of Papa's problems at bay. He had a feeling it was a losing battle. Surely that was why Papa wanted to talk to him.

"You know Mrs. Jones always has a steady supply," Papa said.

Mrs. Jones was better known as Madame Jones. She and her girls lived above Papa's store. When Sidney went to collect for the newspaper, he always tried to peek in and see for himself what went on up there. So far, he'd never been successful. He'd only ever met Mrs. Jones and her maid, Betty.

Sidney took a sip of the drink. Its warmth was comforting going down. He sipped again, then looked at his father's face. Small circles of red spotted Papa's cheeks. No more holding off. Sidney took a deep breath and asked the question he'd been avoiding.

"Papa, what's going on? Why did you have me come here today?"

Papa put a finger to his lips and walked over to the little radio on the counter. He turned up the volume and then came back to where I was standing. "I've come to a decision. I can no longer afford to be—what is it your mama calls me—the dreamer? Yes, my dreams must go."

He looked at the floor. "I have thought about it for a long time. My plan, it is that I'm going to burn down the store."

Sidney flinched. "You're thinking of burning down the store? Are you crazy?"

"Shah!" Papa, looking alarmed, put his fingers to his lips. "This has to be secret between you and me."

Sidney's hands began to shake. He put down the glass of whiskey. "Papa, I can't understand this kind of talk from you. Why would you even think to burn down your store?"

Papa ran his fingers through his sparse salt and pepper hair. "I need the insurance money. To pay bills. To send you and your brother to college one day."

"Papa, I'm fourteen. Sollie's twelve. You don't have to worry about us going to college for a long time."

"Sidneyla, it's not just that."

He gestured around the empty store. "It's the nineteen twenties. Things are changing so fast."

"What does that have to do with anything?"

"I'm just a one-man outfit." Papa shook his head. "People don't come in anymore. They go to Sears. They go to Penney's. My little store is commencing to begin to go down the drain. There's no stopping it."

Sidney stared at his father as if he were a stranger. What kind of world was it that your father came up with such a plan? Yes, they were poor. But they'd always been poor. They'd never been so desperate to break any laws before.

His glance took in the whiskey glass. Papa didn't care about Prohibition laws. Did he feel that way about other laws, too? Sidney wasn't sure anymore. The only thing he knew for certain was he had to talk his father out of this plan.

"Papa, this isn't like you. You'd never hurt anyone or anything. Remember Madame Jones and the girls upstairs in the roominghouse. They could burn to death."

His father smiled. "No they won't. I've thought it all out."

Papa pulled down the shade in the front window and flipped the sign to Store Closed. "Follow me," he said.

He shuffled across the heavily-oiled floor. Sidney, afraid of what his father wanted him to see, lagged behind him. In the back of the store, a ladder leaned against a wall. His father put his foot on the bottom rung and began to climb it. Halfway up, he put his hand out, running it across the bricks. At his touch, one of the bricks moved. Papa pulled it out and placed it on the top of the ladder. He repeated this process with five other bricks.

"Come look," he said.

Sidney didn't need to get on the ladder to see the three shelves that had been hidden by the bricks. A metal moneybox sat on the bottom one. On the middle one there was a white candle in the center of a coil of darkened rope and birch chips.

"See," Papa said, his eyes gleaming. "The candle will burn down to the rope, which I have oiled up really good. This is a fire that will have lots of smoke. Everyone will have plenty warning to get out."

"But, Papa, what if the girls are drunk and don't wake up?" Sidney pointed to the wooden flooring. "With this floor, the store would go up in a flash. And there's only one way down the stairs. You'd be creating a death trap."

"No, that won't happen. I went down by the creek and tried it out. It works, I tell you!"

Sidney's heart pounded. "Papa, you can't be serious. Get money some other way. Run a sale. Go to the bank and get a loan!"

"I already ran a sale, and it didn't do any good. And Mr. Gillespie at the bank said no more loans. No, this is the only way left."

"Then just go bankrupt."

Papa looked scandalized. "I would never do that. Being bankrupt is a terrible thing. Think how it would look for me and my family. Even Mama's people back in Boston would hear about it."

"My God, Papa, going to jail for arson or being hanged for murder is a lot worse."

"Don't worry, my son. Everything will go just fine. I'm not going to get caught."

Sidney stared at his father. Where was the man he thought he knew? A dreamer, yes, but a man with honor. "Papa, you must be out of your mind. How can you talk like this? You always say you hate violence. You can't even cut off the head of a chicken so Mama can fix supper."

"That is disgusting to see the blood. With this, no one will get hurt."

Anger flashed red in Sidney's head, displacing the fear. Mama was right, he realized. Even if he hated hearing her always complaining about Papa, it was true. Papa was an idler who lifted only a little finger when it came to work. If Papa had spent time working on the store and getting customers, they wouldn't be in this fix.

"If you don't stop this crazy talk, I'm going to tell Mama." Sidney's voice held the steel of his determination and the bitterness of his disillusion.

Papa stared at him for a long time. Then he sighed and closed his eyes. He replaced the bricks, one by one, with a careful concentration. He climbed down the ladder like an old man.

When he again stood beside his son, he patted Sidney's arm. "You are right. What have I been thinking? Forget I ever talked to you. I'm just an old stupid fool."

Sidney swallowed hard and nodded. Without another word, he turned and left the store. He had piano to practice and chores to do.

* * *

Over the course of the next few months, Sidney tried to follow his father's advice to forget that the subject of burning down the store had ever been brought up. He was successful most of the time. But they lived near the Whatcom Country Fire Station and once or twice, when the fire engines clanged past their house, Sidney couldn't help thinking of that hidden candle, the coiled rope—and the girls.

One Sunday at four o'clock in the morning, alarm bells from the fire station awakened him. It was almost time for him to get up for his paper route, so he dressed and let himself out the front door. Smoke billowed into the sky from the direction of Old Town.

He ran back inside and up the stairs. He knocked on his parents' door. "Papa," he called, "Papa?"

"Yes, Sidney. What is it?"

Sidney opened the door. His mother and father both sat half-upright in the bed. "What's the matter?" his mother asked.

"There's a fire near Papa's store." Sidney darted a glance at his father, then quickly looked back at his mother. Her eyes were closed now, her hand to her mouth.

"I'll get dressed," Papa said. "You'll come with me, Sidney?"

Sidney nodded and went to wait on the bottom stair. What if it was Papa's store burning? Had Papa followed through on his plan, after all?

They didn't talk as they hurried down the silent streets of their neighborhood. As soon as they reached the outskirts of Old Town, they could smell the smoke. Sidney's feeling of dread increased tenfold. He wasn't surprised to see that Holly Street was blocked by fire engines. Nor was he shocked to see flames shooting from his father's store and the windows above.

"Oh, God," he whispered. He shot his father an accusing look. "Mrs. Jones and her girls."

Papa held up his hands. "Sidneyla, I didn't..."

Sidney cut him off. "I just hope they're all safe. We should pray that none of them are trapped up there."

Papa put a hand on his shoulder, but Sidney shook him off.

He turned away from the fire, sickened by what he saw, and found one of his prayers answered. The Madame, surrounded by women scantily clad in silk robes, stood across the street. She was with Mr. Gillespie, the banker who owned the building. How could they be laughing at a time like this? Sidney wondered.

His father started towards them. Sidney followed.

Betty, Mrs. Jones's maid stood next to her boss, wringing her hands. "It's all my fault. It never would have happened if I was there, but my Charlie was so sick, I just had to go home," she said.

"There, there, Betty. Don't go blamin' yourself. It's not your fault one of the girls fell asleep with a cigarette. I've been warning them, but they never listen. Anyway, we'll be back in business by tomorrow night," Mrs. Jones said. She winked at the banker.

What Mr. Gillespie responded, Sidney never heard. He was pushed from behind and almost fell.

When he regained his balance, he saw a man with a small notebook and pencil moving towards his father. Sidney recognized him as a reporter from the newspaper.

"Hey, Sam," the man called, "what happened?"

Papa talked to the reporter and to Mr. Eriksson, the insurance man, when he arrived. Mr. Gillespie talked to Papa and so did Mrs. Jones. Sidney, it seemed, was the only person in all of Bellingham not talking to him. On the way home, Papa tried to take his hand, but Sidney snatched it away, and ran on ahead.

The next morning when he went to pick up his load of newspapers, Sidney saw the headline. Printed in large letters on the front page were the words, "Burning Cigarette Destroys Old Town Building". He scanned the story—no mention of a candle or arson. For the first time in 24 hours, he managed to take a deep breath. He'd felt so ashamed. Now he stood in the street hawking the newspapers, his head held high.

He saved the last paper to take home. Papa was asleep on the couch when Sidney came in.

"Papa, wake up. See what the newspaper says," Sidney said.

Papa opened one eye and scanned the headlines. A small smile turned up the corner of his lips. Without a word, he rolled over and went back to sleep.

Sidney tiptoed out, smiling too. Papa was going to get the insurance money and he hadn't had to do anything illegal to get it.

* * *

For forty years, they never mentioned the fire again. But in 1962, Papa's kidneys started to fail. Sidney drove up to Bellingham from Seattle in his Rolls Royce to visit.

In the hospital, he was shocked to see how his father had aged in the six months since he'd been there. Papa's skin was yellowed, his face gaunt. Sidney held a glass of water to his lips so he could take a sip.

"Ah, Sidneyla, you're such a good boy. You always were such a good boy."

"Dad, what are you talking about?"

His father gave him a smile. "No matter. Instead, let me tell you something I've wanted to tell you for a long time. Nobody will get hurt now. Most of them are gone."

"Okay, Dad. But don't tire yourself."

"Don't worry, my son. I just want to let you know about the store, when it burned down."

Sidney frowned. "What about it?"

"I never did burn down the store."

"I know. It was a cigarette."

His father shook his head. "No, Sally Jones did it."

"The Madame? But why?"

"Gillespie, the banker, he had built that beautiful Hotel Victoria and wanted Sally to be his partner. The trouble was she had three years left on her lease and she couldn't break it." His father's voice was so weak, Sidney had to lean over to hear him.

"I thought it was Gillespie who owned your building," he said.

"No, it was some old woman. Gillespie's bank held the mortgage."

"Okay, but what makes you think Mrs. Jones was the one?"

His father, even though he lay dying, managed to look cagey. "She told me. One night when her maid was off, she left a white candle burning in one of the rooms." He paused a moment as if to gather his strength. "It took a long time and there was a lot of smoke, but when she saw the flames had caught, she got the girls out."

"You're making that up."

"No, it's true, so help me God." The same little smile lit up his father's face that Sidney remembered from forty years before. He also remembered a white candle and a rope, hidden in a brick wall.

OF PINAFORES AND SATIN BOWS

The summer I was five, I had a lot to worry about. We moved into a new house when my sister was born. Two big adjustments—the house and my sister. But that wasn't all. Every Wednesday at noon an air raid siren went off. President Eisenhower said on the radio that the siren was to help us but it scared me. I had to hold my breath the whole minute so we wouldn't be attacked.

I'd been so happy living at Edgewater, but my parents said three kids couldn't fit into a two-bedroom apartment. I'd loved sharing a room with my big brother, Steve. He knew lots of things, especially how to keep the night monsters away. And I had a million friends. Mother even let me walk to my friend Chi Chi's house by myself.

All that changed at East Boston Terrace. I can't tell you why, but it never felt like a friendly house, even though my parents loved it. "It was designed by the architect Paul Thiry. He's called the father of architectural modernism in the Pacific Northwest, you know," my mother told Auntie Lil, using her Queen of England voice.

In the beginning my sister was in my parents' room. I had my own bedroom and Steve had his. I didn't like it. During the day my wallpaper was a pretty design—bunches of flowers on a blue striped background. But at night the flowers bordering the ceiling turned into skulls and crossbones. My parents were so busy with a new baby, a new store, and a new house that I didn't want to add to their problems. And Steve seemed so far away, even though he was in the next room. So on the nights I felt too scared to close my eyes in case one of the skulls grabbed me, I slept in the hallway.

Then there was the baby. When they first told me about it, I thought a baby in the family might be fun. Boy, was I wrong. First of all, she cried a lot. Second, I thought I'd be able to hold her and maybe feed her a bottle.

After all, I'd had a lot of experience doing it with my doll, but my parents and Allie Mae wouldn't let me near Pamela.

Allie Mae was our maid. We didn't have much money, but, on and off, we had a maid because both my parents worked. They'd bought a jewelry store in downtown Seattle and worked long hours to get it going. It didn't give them much time for anything else. Before the baby, no matter how busy she was, Allie Mae always had time for me. I remember sitting in her lap and playing with her hand. While the outside was brown, the skin of her palm was white, the lifelines darker. I'd trace those lines with my white baby fingers, feeling the softness of her skin and the sandpaper roughness of her fingertips.

But those days of cuddles were gone. Everyone forgot me unless someone said, "Shhhhh, don't wake the baby."

One day I decided I'd had enough. "Daddy," I said, "I don't like how the baby cries. It's so noisy."

My dad patted my head absentmindedly. "Give her a chance, Sarah. If you still don't like your sister, we can mail her back."

"How would you do that?" I asked.

"We'd put her in that big mailbox at the top of the hill."

That gave me pause. She was a pain, all right, but I didn't want Pammy stuffed into a box.

"Okay, I'll give her more time," I said.

After another few weeks I knew it wasn't going to work. "Daddy, I gave her a chance, but now I'm ready to send her back," I said.

Daddy looked up from his newspaper. "Well, the thing is, it's too late now. We can't send her back—we have to keep her."

"But you said we could."

"I know but I can't do anything about it now. If you'd said something sooner..."

I went to bed that night thinking life was so unfair. I was so mad, even the skulls and crossbones didn't bother me.

I wasn't much of an eater in those days. One night Allie Mae put a plate of pot roast, peas, and potatoes in front of me. I could only stare at it. She'd cut up the meat for me, and I finally put a piece in my mouth. I chewed the stringy chunk until it was a glob that I moved from one side of my mouth to the other. "Sugar, you be sure to eat up your roast and those peas, you hear," she said from around the corner of the kitchen.

Swinging my legs, I chewed the beef and worried about how I'd eat the peas. I didn't want the little pea girl to feel lonely as she slid down my throat. I decided to put five peas on my fork so the whole family could go together. Since I couldn't stand the mushy feel of them in my mouth, I began to swallow them whole. But no matter how hard I tried, I could never swallow the meat. It seemed to grow larger until it crowded my tonsils. I spit it into my napkin when Allie Mae wasn't looking. That worked well until she found the wadded-up napkin in the trash can in the bathroom.

"Shame on you. Why, there are starving children in China," she said, swatting my bottom and sending me to my room.

I sat on my bed, hugging my teddy bear and sucking my thumb. Nobody loves me, I thought. Nobody cares.

The next day was Sunday. Daddy always made pancakes and little piggies on Sunday. I got up and started for the stairs. Somehow I tripped and rolled from the top to the bottom. I lay there, unhurt but stunned. Then I started to cry.

"What's the matter?" Daddy called from the kitchen.

My brother came to look. "Oh, she fell down the stairs again," he said. "Come on, baby, get up."

He held out a hand.

"I'm not a baby." I ran back up the stairs to my bedroom.

I got onto my bed and held my teddy tight. The Swensen girls, who lived four houses away, had told me about a girl who knew her family didn't love her.

"She was adopted," Linda said.

"Yeah, and they were mean to her. So she ran away," Barbara added.

I put my thumb in my mouth. Maybe I was adopted. Everyone always asked me where I got my blue eyes because no one else in my family had them. Mommy told me to tell them I got them from the milkman. When I said it, it always got a big laugh. I didn't know why.

Had they wanted to send me back but waited too long and had to keep me? I wondered.

"I bet that's what happened," I said aloud. "Just like with Pammy. They're stuck with me."

I sucked my thumb and thought. Then I stood up. "I better run away like that other girl. They'll be sorry when I'm gone."

In the wardrobe closet I took out my black and white checked case and threw some things in it. I put Teddy under my arm and carefully walked down the stairs.

At the front door I called out, "I'm running away from home."

No one answered. With a heavy heart I opened the door and stepped outside. I walked very slowly out the front yard and past the driveway.

I was sure Mother would come out to scold me for making her nervous. "You get right back into the house this minute!" she'd say.

But no. No one came.

I kept walking, Teddy in one hand and my suitcase in the other. Halfway up the hill I started getting scared. I had no plan. Well, my plan was that someone would stop me. I wasn't allowed to go farther than the top of the hill. And I didn't really want to. I could get lost. Or there could be a bomb. Steve told me if Korea threw a bomb at us, he'd throw it back. But if I was alone, I wouldn't be able to throw it back myself. What was I going to do?

I sat down on the curb and started to cry. I knew it, I thought. No one loves me. Nobody cares about me. They don't even care if I run away. They're probably happy I'm gone.

After a while I trudged back down the hill. I let myself into the house and climbed the stairs as quietly as I could. I didn't want them to know I'd backed down. I unpacked my overnight case and put it away. Then I got under the covers. I held Teddy very close. It was just him and me.

When Daddy tapped on the door and came in, I turned my face into the pillow.

He sat down on my bed. "You're having a tough time, aren't you, Sari?"

I shuddered back a sob but didn't say anything.

"Aww, sweetheart." He began to pat my back. "Don't cry. It'll all work out. You'll see."

The next Saturday, before they left for work, Daddy took me aside. "Sarah, Mommy and I have a real treat planned for you," he said.

"What is it?"

"Steve is going to stay overnight at his friend's. You know, Harvey?"

I nodded. "Uh-huh. He lives by Volunteer Park."

"That's right. So he'll be at Harvey's, and you get to go to Allie Mae's tonight. Then tomorrow you'll spend the whole day with her."

"Really?" I clapped my hands together. "Can I go pack right now?"

He smoothed back my bangs. "Sure can."

In August the sun sets late in Seattle, so even though it was after my bedtime, the sky was bright as we set off from home that night.

Daddy was in the driver's seat, Allie Mae next to him. I was in the back, practicing snapping my fingers. I'd been working on it for a while and was getting close.

It was quiet in the car except for the radio playing a jazzy tune. Every once in a while, I heard Daddy murmur something to Allie Mae.

When we got to her house, it was getting dark. Daddy walked up the wooden stairs onto the porch with us, but I got to carry my suitcase by myself.

"Watch your step here," Allie Mae said, pointing to a place where the wood was splintered.

We walked around the hole to the front door. Allie Mae had her key out and she unlocked it. When we stepped inside, the air felt thick with heat.

Allie Mae turned to my father. "You go on now and don't worry about Sarah. She'll be fine here."

"Okay, but call us if you need to," Daddy said in his worried voice.

She patted his hand. "We won't need anything, Mr. Miller."

Daddy smiled at her and then leaned down to me. "Now, be good and mind Allie Mae."

I put my arms around his neck and he hugged me tight.

By the time he drove off in the Chevy, Allie Mae had rolled up the Venetian blinds to let in a little light.

"Follow me and I'll show you where the bedrooms are," she said.

We walked down a short hallway, and she led me into a bedroom that had pink curtains and a pink bedspread.

"This was my little girl's bedroom," she said.

"Where's your little girl now?"

Allie Mae began turning down the spread. "Ella moved down to Los Angeles."

"Do you miss her?" I asked.

"I do," she said. "I surely do."

I moved over to where she stood and hugged her around the waist.

"You're a sweet child," she said.

In the morning when I opened my eyes, Allie Mae was standing right by my bed.

"I was just going to wake you up," she said. "Breakfast is on the table and we need to hurry. Church starts at ten o'clock."

Breakfast was delicious. Bacon and eggs and something Allie Mae called grits. I ate every bite.

Then Allie Mae took me into the bathroom to clean up. She brushed my hair one hundred strokes and bobbypinned the blue, satin bow into place. She helped me into my white dress and starched blue pinafore she'd ironed at my house. I put on my Mary Janes, which had been polished to a shine with Vaseline.

Allie Mae was already dressed in a gray suit. She pinned her straw hat with the matching gray ribbon into place before she locked the door, and we started down the front stairs.

"Goodness gracious. I don't know how we got so late," she said, hurrying me along the sidewalk.

The church was pretty far away—at least four blocks. When we walked up the stairs and inside, the vestibule was empty. Allie Mae looked me up and down to be sure I hadn't gotten mussed along the way. She refastened the ribbon on my head, and then she pushed open a swinging door. We walked into the church. The walls were painted white, and there was a large cross behind the pulpit in front.

The service hadn't begun yet, but most all of the people sat on benches in rows.

As we started down the aisle, one lady called out, "Allie Mae, is that your sweet little Sarah you talk about?"

I turned to beam at her. She had on a straw hat that was twice as big as Allie Mae's. And it had flowers all over it.

Several people stood and called out greetings as we walked by them. Many touched me on top of my head. Allie Mae smiled more than I'd ever seen her smile.

We moved into an aisle just as the pastor started the service. I liked the way Allie Mae stood so straight, the strap of her pocketbook over her wrist. I liked listening to her voice when she sang the songs.

"They're called gospels," she whispered to me.

I managed to sit quietly for most of the service. Some of the time I practiced snapping my fingers and some of the time the choir sang. When they did, we got to stand up and clap to the music. A woman swayed her arms back and forth so I did too.

The pastor's voice got real loud when he talked, and I scooted closer to Allie Mae. Sometimes people shouted out, "Amen! Amen!" after he said something.

"Amen," I said, trying it out.

When I got fidgety, Allie Mae slipped me a Lifesaver.

After the service Allie Mae led me to the line where people waited to greet the pastor.

Several people patted my head as I came near them.

"Look at those blond curls," a man said.

A woman who had a fur around her neck smiled at me. I leaned into Allie Mae when I saw little fox feet on the fur.

"How sweet," the lady said.

I basked in all the attention, but soon after we'd said our hellos to the pastor, Allie Mae wanted to leave. "Let's go," she said, taking my hand.

As we stood on the sidewalk, she straightened my bow. "I surely didn't like all those people patting your head," she said.

I tilted my head back so I could see her face. "How come?"

"I just didn't," she said.

I knew that voice. It meant I better not ask any more questions.

Because we weren't in a hurry, we walked home at a leisurely pace.

"Look, Allie Mae. A leaf just fell off the tree." I pointed to the brown and green leaf floating to the ground.

She sighed. "It'll be fall before we know it."

She sounded sad so I held her hand tighter.

When we were on Allie Mae's block, I saw a Chevy parked in front of her house.

"Goodness gracious," I said, "my daddy's here."

Allie Mae clutched my hand for a second and then let it go. "Yes, it surely looks like it."

Up ahead the car door opened and Daddy got out.

"Daddy!" I called and ran to his open arms.

He scooped me up and hugged me.

By then Allie Mae had reached us. "Hello, Mr. Miller. I thought Sarah was staying 'til this afternoon."

"We missed her so much, I had to come get her early," Daddy said.

Allie Mae nodded. "I can understand that. Well, come on in while I gather her things together."

Daddy put me down and we followed Allie Mae into the house. Daddy and Mommy missed me, I kept thinking. They missed me!

Allie Mae helped me out of my dress and into play clothes. Then we went into her kitchen, and she packed up fried chicken and potato salad from the refrigerator.

"I'll never eat all this by myself," she said, handing it to Daddy.

When I kissed her good-bye, I thought I saw tears in her eyes. I hugged her extra hard. She must be lonely with her own little girl so far way.

In the car I sat right next to Daddy. "Me and My Shadow" was playing on the radio and we sang along.

At a stoplight he looked over at me. "Did you have a good time?"

I nodded. "It was fun. And all the people in the church were so nice to me."

"Of course they were," Daddy said. "You're a special girl."

I smiled a smile as wide as the ocean.

"I felt Allie Mae was sad that I was leaving," I said after a minute. "I think she misses her daughter."

"I get that. Mommy and I missed you in one day," he said.

As the light turned green, I leaned against his arm. My worries seemed far away.

ONE MOMENT IN TIME

The air was stifling in the small bedroom I shared with my brother. David was gone. *Was he staying overnight at a friend's house or was this the summer they sent him away to military school in Canada? Memory's lens becomes distorted by the sand's flow. The hourglass is not dependable so I can't say for sure. Many other details escape me, too, but the essence of that night has stayed with me through the years. Perhaps it has even sustained me.*

I was probably three-years-old at the time. No more. I clearly remember I was alone in the room and couldn't sleep. August can be hot and sticky in Seattle, and this was one of those years. I had thrown off my blanket, but even the thin sheet weighed on me. The tread of footsteps from the apartment above us shook the ceiling. I could almost trace the path being paced. I began to worry that an evil giant had swallowed the neighbors whole and was planning his next assault, which would be on us.

But this wasn't my only threat. In the corners of the bedroom, the Shadow Monsters began to move. During the day, they were kept under a magic spell and banished. At night, David had the power to keep them at bay. But my brother wasn't there. Emboldened, the monsters slithered out of their caves and loomed at me.

I escaped—fled into the short hall that led directly into our living room. The hardwood floor was smooth under my bare feet as I stood at the threshold peering in. Mother was sitting on the brocade davenport. My mother was beautiful. Her flawless skin, pale porcelain, contrasted dramatically with her black hair. Sometimes, I thought she looked like Snow White—sometimes, like her wicked stepmother.

She stared out the window. She'd been there almost the whole day, motionless. What did she see? I had been careful not to disturb her, playing quietly with my teddy bear on the Persian rug that was threadbare in spots. When Daddy came home from work, he fixed dinner and made Mother sit at the table with us. She didn't eat, didn't even pick up her fork.

Daddy spooned mashed potatoes on my plate next to the chicken and peas. "Do you know, I heard at work today that Eisenhower is going to send more troops to Korea," he said.

Mother said nothing. I didn't either. I had heard of Korea on the radio that sat on the credenza next to the fireplace. Korea was a bad place with many monsters. They had bowling balls there that they could light the ends of. When they threw them, the balls exploded with a loud *pssssst*.

I ate most of my dinner, except for the peas because they took so much time. I had to separate them into pea families and swallow the group together. I worried that the little girl pea would get separated from her mother and father and brother. She could end up by herself in the cavern of my stomach. Who would take care of her?

When it was time for me to go to bed, Daddy had helped me brush my teeth and read me two stories. I loved to hear the rise and fall of his voice.

"Mother is having trouble coping with things," Daddy told me when he tucked me in. He kissed me on the forehead and lightly touched my face.

I heard him sigh a couple of times as he drew the drapes, leaving the window open a crack for air. He didn't look back at me when he closed the door behind him.

Was it my fault? I wondered as I lay in the darkening room. Did I cause my mother to have trouble doing this coping? I had a feeling I did. I knew I was a lot of work for my parents—their constant weariness would have eased if I hadn't required attention. They were older than other parents—they called me their surprise baby.

Now, here I was, still awake. Still awake, and afraid to be alone. Still not letting them be. I could see Daddy across the room from Mother. He sat at the upright piano, playing either Beethoven or Chopin, the melancholy motif apparent. His curved fingers moved above the piano keys so he wouldn't disturb the silence. I was quiet, too, but he heard me and turned.

"I need a glass of water, Daddy," I said when he spied me in the shadows. "I'm so thirsty."

He stilled for a moment. Then he smiled the kindest smile I have ever seen. It held humor and understanding…and love. "Go get your sneakers, Sarah," he said, getting up from the piano bench. "And I'll get you a drink."

I ran back to my room and flipped on the light. That vanquished the monsters! I was dragging my shoes out of the closet when Daddy came in with the water. He tied my shoes, and tousled my wispy curls.

"Let's walk to Uncle Sol's," he said.

We lived in an apartment complex called Edgewater—New England-style brick buildings that sprawled along the edge of Seattle's Lake Washington. My aunt and uncle lived six blocks away. To walk that far with my dad would be an adventure. To be alone with him was a treasure beyond compare.

Daddy took my hand, and we tiptoed out, leaving Mother still staring. I worried for a moment about her, but didn't linger. I was anxious to escape with my prize before it was taken from me.

Outside, it was not as dark. Safely away, we shook off the sepia gloom of the apartment. We strolled along, me in my Carter rosebud pajamas and Daddy in his shirtsleeves, a definite jauntiness in our step. We passed the building next to ours. Raised voices blared out of an open window. I moved closer to Daddy.

Two more blocks and we were past the bus stop with its wooden enclosure, where other monsters lurked. Sometimes, when we waited for the bus, the rain drummed so loudly on the tin roof that I had to put my hands over my ears. But, tonight the sky was clear, a silver-sapphire as the light leached away. The twilight painted the street rosy—the World War II houses glowed in the pipe-tobacco-scented air.

I smiled and took a little skip, unable to contain my joy.

I was with my daddy. He was with me. For this one moment in time, he seemed to need no more.

Piece Of Cake

In the sun's afternoon assault, heat shimmered over the street, undulating like a sheet of liquid glass. Sara felt sweat gather at the hollow of her throat and trickle between her breasts. On the radio, they said it was going to be 108. She believed it.

She'd felt nauseous all day. She felt dizzy, now, standing out where there wasn't any shade, but she couldn't go inside. Her father and his girlfriend were coming over to visit. It was only polite that she be out front when they got there.

She rubbed her temples. "Please God, let it be soon."

She'd had a tooth extracted two days before. They'd told her she'd be fine by the weekend. But she wasn't. She wished she'd said she didn't feel up to company, but she hated to say no to her father. He was 92. At his age, you couldn't afford to lose any chance to be together.

She closed her eyes against the black dots encroaching her vision. "You can do this," she whispered into the desert stillness. "You know how to endure anything." That at least was true. She'd become an expert at endurance.

When she felt safe to open her eyes, she saw Barbara's black SUV coming down the empty street. She put a smile on her face and waved.

As soon as they parked, Sara walked over to open the passenger door. "Hi, Dad, It's great to see you."

Her father's only answer was a brief nod. His gnarled fingers groped for the safety strap and he inched himself to the edge of the seat.

When had his movements become so tentative, so stiff?

"Do you want some help, Dad?"

"No, I can do it myself."

She heard the touchiness in his voice, was expecting it. His pride was what kept him going, but she always asked anyway.

He slid forward so his feet reached the running board, then paused before stretching his legs further. A gust of wind flapped the material of his pants against his legs.

When had he gotten so thin?

"Hi, Sara, how're you doing?" Barbara's cheerful voice cut across Sara's pensive thoughts.

Her father's girlfriend was Sara's age, 52. This engendered many gold digger comments from her father's friends, but Sara didn't believe it for a minute. Barbara was too kind, too open to be out for Dad's money.

"Good, I'm feeling good," Sara said. "Let's go in through the garage. It's shorter than going around to the front door."

Sara led them into the relative coolness of the garage. Behind her, she could hear her father's labored breathing and his unsteady step.

Why wouldn't he use the cane they'd bought him at the Antique Show?

"Wow, look at your new car—a Jaguar!" Barbara said. "It's gorgeous."

Sara looked back. Barbara was opening the car door. "And that new car smell." Barbara inhaled loudly. "Nothing like it. "

Sara gave her an uneasy look. She loved her new car, the way it looked and the way it drove, but Barbara's comments embarrassed her.

"That's quite a fancy, car, daughter," Sara's father said.

Sara's embarrassment flared to something more. "Yes, but it's not a regular Jaguar. And we didn't buy it. We leased it. It was such a great deal." The words came out defensive, apologetic.

"Well, whatever, it's gorgeous. You're a lucky girl." Barbara held out a Saxe Fifth Avenue shopping bag. "I'm so excited. We brought you a little present and it will go perfectly with your new car."

"You got me a present?" Sara smiled.

"Yeah, your daddy and I got you something, but I bet you already have at least one."

"I don't know about that, but it's so nice of you to think of me. I can't tell you how good it makes me feel. Come on, I'll open it up inside."

Sara held the door for them.

"You mean Hank didn't get you anything?" Barbara asked as she walked past.

"Oh, right." Sara rolled her eyes. "He says I only had a tooth pulled, not major surgery. He doesn't understand why I couldn't play in the golf tournament with him. He can't believe I'm as bruised up as I am."

"Really? He's not the most sympathetic guy in the world, is he? Is he here?"

For some reason, Barbara's remarks about Hank annoyed Sara. "No, out golfing as usual," she answered, her tone light.

Conversation ceased until they were in the sun lit living room. "Oh, my God, Sara, look at your face," her father said. He held her chin. "Oh, my God," he repeated.

"Let me see." Barbara crowded next to him. "That's terrible. You look like those pictures of Nicole Brown Simpson. You know the ones she put in a vault to show how vicious O.J. could be."

"Maybe I should have you take a couple of pictures of me like this. I could always pull them out and scare Hank if he gets out of line," Sara joked.

"Maybe you want to use the pictures to sue the oral surgeon," Barbara said.

"Why would I do that?"

"You're so swollen and black and blue. That can't be right."

Sara looked at her dad. "I'm making a tooth drama just like Mother would have. Right, Dad? Didn't she bruise like this?"

He nodded. "Just like that."

"That's what I thought." Sara turned to Barbara. "I get bruises just making the bed, so for me this is no big deal. Besides, with all this swelling I can get a preview of what I'd look like with a face-lift. See, on the swollen side of my mouth—voila, no wrinkles!"

"The before and after—all on one face," Barbara said.

Sara laughed and then rubbed her jaw. "Ouch, don't make me laugh. It hurts." She blinked away another wave of dizziness. "Come on, sit down. Can I get you something to drink?"

Barbara settled onto the couch, Sara's dad next to her. "No, we just finished lunch," he said.

"All right, we'll just visit, then." Sara sank down on the love seat across from them.

"Your house looks so nice." Barbara's eyes flitted to all the corners of the room.

"Thanks. I'm glad we decided to redecorate. Everything seems so much fresher, now," Sara said.

"And your fireplace looks so different refinished. That must have cost a bundle."

Sara felt uncomfortable again. Sometimes Barbara could get too close to the line. She knew Barbara's ex-husband had been a jerk who'd gambled away all their money. Barbara had barely got a settlement from him. Sara, on the other hand, had been married thirty years to Hank who'd invested their money conservatively. Now with both kids graduated from college, they'd begun to spend on themselves a little more. Why, all of a sudden, did she feel like it was a crime?

"No," Sara said, "refinishing the fireplace wasn't bad, at all. Wouldn't have done it, if it were. This artist who's just moved to Palm Springs from LA came in and painted it."

"Just beautiful, Sara. Just like you are," Barbara said. "Or were, before that doctor beat the hell out of your face. Now come on, open your gift. It's perfect for you."

"Okay." Sara pulled the box out of the bag and untied the ribbon. She'd never received many gifts as a child, so she still loved opening packages.

"Oh, what a great looking hat," she said, pulling the lilac colored cap out of the tissues. "And look, it's got a place to put your key when you're walking."

"See, Jack, I told you she'd like it," Barbara said. "Sara, you're sure you don't already have one?"

"Not with a place for a key." Sara looked at a card tucked into the inside of the cap. "What's this say? I don't have my glasses."

"It says PRADA."

Sara looked up. "You're kidding, right?"

Barbara shook her head. "Nope."

"A Prada baseball cap? A real Prada? Not a fake?"

"A real one," Barbara said.

"Prada? I'm sorry, I don't want to be rude, but how much did this cost, fifty bucks?" Sara asked.

Barbara pointed her thumb upward.

"Not a hundred?" Sara asked.

"No, more," Sara's father said.

Sara was horrified. She used baseball caps to walk every day. They got sweaty and dirty fast. They had labels like Nike on them, nothing designer, for God's sake. "Just how much?"

"Two hundred and eight dollars," Barbara answered triumphantly.

Sara's sore jaw dropped. Her father had spent two hundred bucks on a baseball cap? All the years of birthdays without a wrapped gift, and now he'd bought her a ten-buck item for two hundred dollars? Jesus!

"I'm sorry. I can't keep this." Sara stuffed the hat back into the box. Barbara frowned. "But why not?"

"It's too much money for a cap that's going to be sweat-stained in two days." Sara smiled to soften her words. "I love it that you thought of me, but I have to take it back."

"But you're a princess," Barbara said, gesturing with her arm to encompass the living room. "Look at how you live. Look at all the things you have."

Sara surveyed the paintings, the pieces of Steuben and Lalique, the Limoges box collection, the furniture. What she saw was thirty years of anniversary and birthday presents. The painting of the roses was paid for by the vacation they hadn't taken two years ago. The figurines on the fireplace were part of the antiques that no one else in the family had wanted. This room held a history for Sara, a combination of love, strife, and a desire for balance.

"You think I'm a princess, Barbara? What does that mean? That I'm spoiled and not willing to get down and do the dirty work? I'm telling you, there's nothing farther from the truth."

"No, I don't think you're spoiled or selfish. You're just dainty and you always look good and you have such nice things."

Sara examined Barbara, trying to see in her face the meaning behind her words. "I don't know what you're talking about. All I can say is, I'm no princess."

"But I want you to be," Barbara said. "I want you to wear that hat."

Sara rubbed her throbbing temple and glanced at her father who had folded his arms across his chest. His eyes were closed.

Was he dozing or just withdrawing from the conversation? Was his hearing aid even still on?

"The last thing on earth I'd ever want to be is a princess. And I was raised to be the worker bee in my family, anyway."

"What do mean?" Barbara asked.

"I don't want to go into ancient history, but I've been taking a memoir class and it seems to be dredging up old memories. I just wrote a story about my mother cutting pieces of cake for my sister and me when I was about five. One piece was larger and I naturally grabbed for that one. Mother said, 'How can you be so selfish and take the bigger piece? You should give it to your little sister.' I remember standing there with that piece of cake in my hand, looking at it, at my mother, at my baby sister and back again."

Sara paused to catch her breath. Were her dad's eyes still so tightly closed? Was he listening? "I know I wavered for at least a minute before I made my decision. I was the biggest so why shouldn't I have the biggest piece? And I was the first in line. Wasn't I entitled to first choice? Why couldn't my mother have made the pieces more equal? It didn't seem fair, but in the end, I gave the bigger piece to my sister and took the smaller one for myself."

"What a crock. Your mother was a piece of work," Barbara said.

Sara shrugged. "Maybe, but that little cake episode changed my entire personality and my life. Yeah, I wanted the bigger piece, but I wanted my mother's approval more. I have pictures from that time…a few years before. I was a feisty looking little kid. But from then on, I changed. I watched my every move to see my mother's reaction.

"From then on, I ate chicken legs, not because I liked them, but because that's what was left on the platter. I tried harder and harder to please my mother and my dad. I studied so hard I got A's when I was only really a B student. I cleaned and cooked and took care of my sister. But nothing was ever enough. So I started reading. In my books, I could escape. I didn't have to be me…the one who couldn't quite measure up, no matter how much I did."

The air conditioner came on. Sara started at the noise and stopped talking. She looked down at her hands and saw they were shaking. She folded them quickly into her lap. Barbara must think she was an idiot, revealing all that bull shit from her childhood.

At the feel of the softness of her father's hand on hers, Sara looked up. He stood over her with tears in his eyes. "I never knew about your mother and the cake," he said.

Sara's eyes also filled with tears. How many years had she waited for her dad to acknowledge her like this? It felt as if he were seeing her for the first time. She should be feeling gratified, but she felt only sad. "Doesn't matter. Like I said, it's ancient history. Just wish the hell I could get over it, and start feeling that I am entitled to the best and the biggest."

"Then keep the hat," Barbara said.

"No way. But when I return it, I'll look around for something for myself," Sara said.

"Good." Her father gingerly straightened. "Now, we're going to get out of here and let you rest. You look exhausted."

"All this high drama does wear on one," Sara said.

After they had gone, Sara carefully wrapped the hat back into the tissue, closed the box and retied the ribbon. Just looking at the hat, made her shudder. What a waste of money.

Why was Barbara so insistent that she have the hat? Was it Barbara who had wanted it for herself? The idea came to her as she started to straighten the pillows on the couch.

She thought about her father sitting there with his eyes closed. That had felt familiar. In her childhood, he'd often withdrawn, she realized now. Her mother had been so difficult, and her dad didn't like confrontation.

"So we kids were left on her own, hanging in the wind," she said aloud. "To deal with that crazy woman."

Maybe her father hadn't known about the cake, or maybe he had. But the truth was, it didn't matter. Her mother was dead and her father was who he was. It really was time she got over it.

After she'd taken a pain pill, she lay down on her bed, her body folding itself into the covers. When she closed her eyes, a vision of her dad in all his frailness appeared before her. And next to him was Barbara, wearing the Prada hat and in the driver's seat of her dead mother's car.

She sat up. And even though it hurt her mouth, she laughed.

THE PAIL OF WATER

When he wouldn't empty the pail of water, something snapped in Laura. At the time, she just gritted her teeth, gritted them so hard her jaw and head would ache for the next two days. Even though she never swore, she muttered under her breath, "You son of a bitch," and emptied the pail, herself.

It was a Sunday at the beginning of June and Laura was cleaning house. Unseasonable heat hung over the LA Basin like an electric blanket on high. The air outside smelled like car exhaust—the air inside moved only by way of the fan set up on the television in front of Laura's husband. Brian's hair blew to one side like graying stalks of yellowed corn in an October wind. Stretched out on the brown vinyl couch, he didn't seem to hear Laura's sighs or the sounds of brush against wood as she scrubbed the floor around him. He watched a double header on the 35-inch screen, his full mouth set in lines of habitual discontent, as if she didn't exist.

Five feet eight and pencil thin, Laura was pale from teaching too many hours, from taking care of the house and kids; from not having time to remember who she'd been, let alone recognize who she'd become. She never thought about the young college graduate who had set off to change the course of American history. That girl, eyes bright with hope and confidence, would be a stranger to her, now. But twenty years ago, the ideal that education was the key to unlocking the gates of the inner city had kept Laura going. True, the light in her eyes dimmed with the reality of the apathy and anger, which crippled her teenage students. But it was only when Brian, her husband of six months, ridiculed her dedication that she had begun to doubt herself.

"For Christ's sake, Laura, what're you trying to do? You're fighting a losing battle," he'd said, licking the spot behind her ear that sent sensual arrows down her spine, instantly hardening her nipples. She'd been correcting papers when he pulled her towards him. He rubbed his erection against her pelvis, lifting her off her feet. Almost faint with desire, she followed him to bed, leaving her work unfinished.

She had always scoffed at people who said they were madly in love—until she met Brian. Then she learned the truth of the expression. Shivering from his lightest touch, Laura wanted to do what pleased him. Still she was convinced that her teaching could make a difference. She kept at it through the bomb threats and marijuana-bombed kids, but when a protest group set the school on fire, Brian made her quit.

"I don't want any wife of mine to be around that much danger." He'd splayed his hand wide to run it down her soft back. She'd been chubby then, still protected by a layer of baby fat.

"And besides," he whispered in her ear, "don't you want to start a family?"

Although she'd just been promoted to head of her department, Laura finished up the school year and turned in her resignation. Enveloped in a haze of sensuality and love, she'd felt that Brian's words were a pledge of his love and regard of her. Dutifully, but with joy, she'd gotten pregnant with their son.

In the hospital after Michael's birth, she'd inspected his tiny perfect toes and fingers. Her eyes shone again, this time like sun lighted pebbles in a shallow stream. "Isn't he a miracle, Brian?" she said with awe, her smooth cheeks plump, her breasts rounded with the fullness of creation.

When he didn't answer, she looked up. Brian's scowl, an increasingly familiar sight, was directed at her. What had she possibly done wrong, now?

"A miracle? Christ, Laura, babies are born every fuckin' day." He held up the hospital bill. "What's a miracle is how we'll be able to afford him!"

Pumped full of after-birth endorphins, Laura was unfazed by his vitriolic tone. She smiled at him with Madonna-like wisdom. "Oh, come here, Mr. Grumpy." She extended her free arm out to him. "Come see this handsome young fullback you've sired."

Like a sulky child, Brian approached the bed. Laura ignored the expression on his face, instead watching how the light from the window made the strands of his blond hair glisten. She squeezed his large, square hand and pulled him down beside her on the bed. He trailed a finger lightly over Michael's cheek, his face softening as he looked at the baby suckling at her breast.

"I'd like to be doing that right now." Brian winked at her, then gave her the cocky smile, which always charmed her. "Tell my greedy son to move over," he teased. He continued to gently touch Michael's soft baby head with one hand, but cupped her breast with the other.

Laura sighed back into the pillows, relieved that another of Brian's black moods had been headed off. She felt uncomfortable with him fondling her cantaloupe-sized breasts right in the open. Anyone walking down the hospital corridor might see them, but she was reluctant to ask him to stop, afraid he'd blow up at her.

As the years went by, Brian's volatility increased, and his dark moods lingered. Only rarely did his charm surface. Laura tried to anticipate his reactions to avoid any trouble. Harmony was so important to her that she'd do anything to keep her home peaceful. Her parents had fought almost non-stop until they'd finally divorced—she'd never gotten over her fear of their rages.

Determined to save Michael, and then his sister, Ashley, from the same anxiety-laden atmosphere, she worked hard to make everything perfect so Brian would find no reason to become upset. "Children," she'd say at 5:00 each evening, "pick up your toys and go to your rooms, now. Daddy will be home soon and he doesn't like a mess. And remember to be quiet. Daddy doesn't like noise."

A deep frown line grew on her forehead, furrowing her brow like a newly plowed field. Sometimes, kernels of anger sprouted in her, but she would bury them quickly as deep as she could. She felt guilty about her resentment, vowing to be a better wife and housekeeper. She'd never been successful at making her father happy. Now she was failing her husband.

When Ashley was nine, the recession hit them hard. Laura returned to teaching to help the family finances. Because she'd never finished her Masters, she started at a low pay scale. Brian berated her for how little she earned, but Laura tried to understand. She knew he was bitter that he, alone, could not support his family. This, she felt, made him angrier and on edge. She and the children trod even more carefully around him, never knowing when he'd erupt.

Michael, thirteen now, told Laura that his father was like the Kilauea volcano. "Sometimes calm and sometimes so much fun, more fun than anyone," he said. "Then watch out! Red-hot lava! And if you don't want to burn, you'd better get out of the way fast." Laura laughed at the metaphor until she cried.

Brian's temper escalated with rumors that the bank, where he was a manager, was going to be bought out. Although he never hit her, he had knocked her glasses off her nose once. And she sometimes had to wear a scarf to hide the imprint his fingers made when he wrapped his hands around her neck and squeezed.

"You're a useless bitch," he'd shouted as she flinched from his raised hand. He'd slammed out of the house, not returning until late at night. Laura, awake, but feigning sleep, had held herself stiffly on her side of the bed. It was only when she heard him weeping like a child that she'd turned towards him.

"Brian, what's the matter?"

"Oh, God, Laura." He threw his arms around her and burrowed his head into her flat breasts. "Baby, my life is going down the drain. If the other bank comes in, I know they'll fire me. Then what will I do?"

"Shhhhush, shush," she crooned, smoothing his Robert Redford hair away from his eyebrows. "It'll be fine, just you wait. They won't fire you. Things will work out. They always do."

Laura was wrong about Brian's job. He did lose it. Not sleeping, not dressing or shaving, he smoked his way through the days, too depressed to even go on-line, a pastime he had previously spent hours at. "Why do I have such bad luck?" he'd mutter as in lay in bed. "I've tried hard all my life, and this is what I get? Why is this happening to me?"

Laura watched him, wringing her hands, not knowing what to do. When she suggested he go to one of the recruiting companies he shouted at her, "I'm a fucking failure, okay? Just leave me the hell alone. Stop nagging!"

Laura took on two tutoring jobs to help keep the family afloat and pay off her graduate degree loans. Completely exhausted, she'd been glad that Brian hadn't approached her for sex. But lately, he wanted to make love nightly and sometimes in the afternoon. She started staying later at school to avoid him—Brian now wanted the sex to be quick and hard. It made her feel like a vending machine.

At school, her principal called her in. She was sure it was to chastise her for poor performance. Instead he offered her the job of assistant principal for the coming year. There would have to be a selection committee and interviews, but with his recommendation, it was simply a formality. Stunned, but thrilled, Laura drove over the speed limit to get home to share the news with Brian.

His reaction devastated her. "You sleeping with him? That why you've been so late coming home?" he asked.

"Of course not!" Laura let her anger loose for once. "Why would you think that?"

Brian looked her up and down. "I just was wondering why he'd offer you the job, that's all."

She walked out of the room, her fists tightly clenched, her back rigid. Sometimes, she thought, Brian went too far.

Sick all night with stomach pains, by morning she had decided Brian might be right. Maybe the principal did expect illicit payment for her promotion. She wasn't really that qualified, was she? At school, taut with confusion, she hid in her classroom, eating lunch at her desk. When she got home, she found Brian in the kitchen making dinner.

Shaved and in clean clothes, he smiled at her. "Thought I'd help out a little."

He drew her to him, and kissed her nose. "Why don't you go rest a bit, Baby, and I'll have Ash call you when dinner's ready."

Later that night, after a long, slow lovemaking, which had Laura spiraling as high as she'd ever been, Brian snuggled her close. "I didn't mean to upset you last night," he whispered. "I just get worried that a job like assistant principal might be too much for you."

Inhaling the smell of soap and his maleness, her thighs still sticky with his sperm, Laura smiled into his naked shoulder. Brian really cared about her, she told herself. He might not be tactful, but he cared. He wanted to protect her. She felt sure that he loved her as much as she loved him. So what if he was moody? He had good reason. She knew that she'd stay by his side forever.

But everything changed on the Sunday that Brian wouldn't empty the pail of water. Resentment rose in her like bile. It flowed into her veins, flooding her body. Her shoulders ached as she picked up the bucket, carried it outside and flung the soapy contents onto the lawn. "I hope it kills the grass," she ground out through her teeth.

She stood still a moment, letting the sun beat down on her, along with the truth. If Brian wouldn't do the smallest thing she asked, his love for her was as thin as the blades of grass she stood on. And if he didn't care for her, care what she needed, what had the last seventeen years been about? She wanted to scream and keep on screaming. Instead, because she didn't want to frighten Michael and Ashley, she just gritted her teeth and went back into the house.

It wasn't until past midnight that her armor of anger dissipated. Dressed only in a faded cotton nightgown, she sat in front of the fan, attempting to read a Martha Grimes mystery. On page 135, she followed what Richard Jury said to Melrose Plant. On page 136, the words swam in front of her eyes, obscured by tears. Her sobs, which began as a soundless shaking of her shoulders, grew in waves until she could no longer contain her anguish. Keening notes of despair escaped her. Her arms wrapped around her middle, she rocked back and forth.

Brian's concerned face as he stormed into the room did nothing to deter her cries of bereavement.

"My God, Laura, what's the matter?" He crouched next to her. "Baby, are you hurt?"

Laura studied his face, looking at him as if he were a stranger. How could he be so unaware? she wondered. Didn't he know how he'd hurt her?

"Laura, honey, talk to me. Tell me what's the matter. You can't go on like this."

Heartened by the genuine concern she heard in his voice, Laura allowed her heart to re-open just a crack. Maybe, she thought, I'm wrong. Maybe he does care. Maybe I should have shown him how I've felt before this. "You wouldn't empty the pail of water," she whispered.

Brian reared back from her. "You're carrying on because I wouldn't empty the fuckin' pail?"

"Don't shout. You'll wake the kids."

"You're the one who's been moaning loud enough to wake the dead." Brian grabbed her arm. "You're crazy, Laura, you know that? I think you've finally gone 'round the bend like your mother."

He glared at her, his upper lip slanted at an angle, displaying his incisor teeth. It was a look that had terrified her for years. Now she only noticed, with some fascination, that his teeth were beginning to yellow. She closed her eyes and resumed rocking back and forth.

"And why the fuck should I empty the goddam bucket? I didn't fill it, did I?" The pressure of Brian's fingers tightened enough to still her rocking.

She opened her eyes, but didn't look at him. "I don't ask you for much, Brian. I've never asked for much. And when I was so tired, and you were just watching television, it didn't seem like emptying the pail would be that much . . ."

"Jesus Christ! You're making a big deal out of nothing, a fuckin' mountain out of a molehill!" The veins in Brian's neck stuck out.

She backhanded the fresh tears falling down her cheeks. "You hurt me, Brian, so much. I swear my heart is breaking."

"Oh, your heart is breaking," he mimicked.

His sarcasm was like a torch. It ignited a rage that dried her tears. She looked at Brian's chest where his heart should have been, and longed for a knife so she could stick it deep into that spot.

She got up from the couch, her movements slow and precise. Skirting Brian, intent on not touching him, she started for the door.

"Where are you going?""

When she didn't respond, Brian shouted, "Answer me, dammit!"

She turned. "I told you to be quiet. The children do not need to hear this."

"Don't you dare talk to me in that tone." His voice was heavy with threat.

"I'm not afraid of you, Brian. Not anymore. You don't like this tone, then get out." She paused. "Yeah, get out or get used to it because I'm done walking on egg shells around you. I've had it up to here," she said, gesturing at her throat, "with your bull shit."

Brian looked startled, whether it was because she had stood up to him or sworn, Laura didn't know. Neither did she care.

In the hallway, she could see a light on in Michael's room, and the door open to Ashley's. They were probably huddled together, frightened by what they were hearing. She should go to them, but what could she say?

Lying in bed, with the bedroom door locked, she didn't attempt to sleep. Instead, she went over all the incidents, the days and years of Brian treating her as if she didn't matter. She pounded the mattress with her fists as she remembered all he'd said to belittle her—all he'd done to show his disregard for her needs. She, who hated clichés, had been one—the typical battered wife. Like the ones she'd listened to on the NPR series. Only she had been beaten with words instead of fists.

It was a long time before she slept. When she did, she dreamed she was in a huge house that was all in white. There were many people there, men and women who were killing each other and hiding the bodies. Laura was afraid she'd be caught in the house and blamed for the killings. A woman took off her wig, revealing her bald head. Then parts of her face came off. She was pale white under the make up. "Aren't you afraid people will see you like this," Laura asked her. The woman shrugged and pulled off more skin. Other people committed murder in the dream, cutting up body parts and putting them down the toilet. But Laura could see the parts coming back up, a shoulder—an arm. She woke, sweating, not remembering all the details of the dream, but feeling the fear.

Brian was asleep on the couch when she went downstairs. In the kitchen, the children had already poured themselves cereal and sat at the table.

"You okay, Mom?" Michael's expression was anxious.

Laura nodded and smiled. "I smell coffee."

'We made you some," Ashley said.

"Thanks, guys." Laura went over to the counter and poured coffee into a mug.

"Mom, your eyes are all puffy and red," Ashley said when Laura sat down with them.

Laura reached over and put her arm around Ashley's thin shoulders. "I'm sure you must have heard Dad and me fighting last night."

Both children nodded their heads, looking like puppets afraid they had lost their puppeteer.

"Don't look so worried, guys. It's going to be okay." Laura sighed. "I understand a lot more now, than I did yesterday."

"Are you and Daddy going to get a divorce?" Ashley asked.

She looked at her kids. "I don't know the answer to that. I can honestly tell you I have no plans to leave Dad."

And she meant it. She knew how painful it was for kids when their parents split, and she didn't want that for Mike and Ashley. But never again would Brian have the same power. She could never feel the same about him. A part of her had died, just as in her dream. But other parts had been reborn.

She rubbed her jaw, sore from gritting her teeth. She would apply for the assistant principal job. With calm objectivity, she could see how her years of teaching and her Masters in Administration indisputably qualified her. More than that, she would insist Brian start looking for a job.

Yes, for now she'd stay with him for the kids, and truth be told, because a part of her still loved him. Even last night when his callous disregard was the source of her pain—the brush of his skin against hers' had felt like velvet, soft, precious and necessary.

She gritted her teeth again. Life was so confusing—it was hard to know what to do.

Then she straightened her shoulders. "We'll be fine kids," she said, looking at each of them in turn. "Whatever happens, we'll be fine."

POWER PLAY

The throb of Jimi Hendrix's guitar filled the room as Richard measured out the half cup of Parmesan he'd grated earlier. He loved the music, but loved the contrast even more—Seventies rock and roll played from Sirius Radio through state-of-the-art 21st century equipment. Perfect.

The sound hit the Frankenthaler and Pollock abstracts that hung on the ochre walls, setting off a concussion of sound and sight that filled Richard with a sense of vitality. He'd been around to witness Jimi Hendrix concerts and the Expressionist Era, and he was still alive and thriving. He might be in his sixties, but he was a man of the new millennium.

Richard took a taste of the Parmigiano-Reggiano. The cheese's fermentation process added a kick he found delicious. That Jessica thought it too strong was her problem, not his.

Deftly dicing the hothouse tomatoes, he tossed them and the cheese into the salad greens. He washed his hands, then picked up the bottle of olive oil set at right angles to the chopping board. He poured oil into a bowl, adding freshly squeezed lemon juice. A pinch of salt and a generous serving of chopped garlic finished the dressing. He whisked the ingredients together, and dipped his finger into the mixture for a taste.

The tartness of the lemon puckered his mouth. "Perfect," he said.

He liked things that way—perfect. He insisted on it at home and in the office. From an early age, he'd learned to plan and make decisions to get him exactly what he wanted. And he'd always had the balls to discard what no longer worked. It was all in the art of making the perfect deal.

He rolled his shoulders, loosening the tension from his neck. Cooking was a balm to him—a sure way to soothe his nerves. He made dinner three nights a week. Jessica told everyone it was because she demanded it. Let her think she had such power over him. Anyone who really knew Richard understood he only did what he wanted.

After he put the salad in the refrigerator to chill, he began washing the utensils he'd used. He paused a moment, the wire whisk suspended from his fingers as he thought about Jessica. She could be relentless in getting what she wanted. He had no problem with that, but now he felt an on-going undercurrent between them—a struggle for control. Her new thing was a push to move out of their downtown Seattle condo to a big house in the suburbs. "Been there, done that," he muttered.

He stared at his reflection in the kitchen window. The eyes of a man who was shrewd and tough stared back. He was proud of that incisive expression, just as he was proud of his thick head of silvered hair, his tanned and taut body. He worked hard to keep himself mentally and physically fit—always had. That along with careful planning and analysis had made him pretty much disaster proof. So many people he knew had crashed along with the economy in 2008. He was making more money than ever.

Life was on his terms. If things weren't right, he made them that way. Like when he found out Diana was cheating on him. He'd been hurt, sure, but not humiliated. The tawdry affair with her ski instructor had been an embarrassing cliché, nothing more. He not only weathered her defection, he grew stronger from it. When he met Jessica, he'd been divorced for two years. He'd dated some, but investment banking was a demanding lover—work had taken most of his time. Jumping into the whirlwind that surrounded Jessica had been refreshing and stimulating at the same time.

For the first few years, he reveled in the lifestyle that was similar to his own sons'—the snowboarding in Aspen in winter, the waterskiing in the Lake Tahoe summer home, the golf and tennis all over the world. He even loved the constant clubbing—the dancing, the noise, the Mohitos—the frenetic energy that so defined Jessica. But, if he were totally honest with himself, it was losing its appeal. Worse, he felt he had to be constantly on his toes—that if he let down, he'd lose ground.

He had come to these realizations about a month before. Jessica and he were in Dubai, staying at the Burj Al Arab hotel. His business concluded, they'd celebrated with champagne and caviar in their suite, which was as large as the house he'd grown up in. Satiated for a moment, either with her drawn-out orgasms or the luxury of the seven-star hotel, Jessica had fallen asleep beside him on the sheik-sized bed.

In the silence, he'd come up against an unwelcome truth. Instead of feeling triumphant at his skilled negotiating, he felt nothing. He looked at his forty-year-old wife with her perfect body, and also felt nothing. Just relief that she was asleep, and he didn't have to talk to her. Sometimes he yearned for a conversation with someone who actually remembered the day John F. Kennedy was shot, and didn't think of it as a historical event. Jessica had read Stephen King's *11-22-63* for her book club and kept pestering him with questions about those days like he was her own personal Wikipedia. It made him feel like a relic.

He frowned. Was he getting maudlin? Was that what happened to people who hit sixty? He obliterated that awful notion by turning on the faucet full steam. He gave the whisk a vigorous shake and set it on the drain board. It was unlike him to let negative thoughts get him down. It had to be the phone call he'd received a half hour ago. It put a different light on his marriage. More than that, it pointed out his immediate need to reassess.

"Oh, Richard. You are here."

Richard looked over his shoulder. Jessica stood in the doorway, a weary expression on her face.

"I didn't hear you come in. I guess because the water was on."

"You're home early," she said, leaning against the doorframe. "You texted that you'd be late."

He shrugged. "I put the Claremont deal to bed by two o'clock. Had a late lunch with them, and decided, what the hell, might as well come home, and see my gorgeous wife."

"But I wasn't here."

"Yeah. You weren't here." He dried his hands with the jade-green kitchen towel, not looking at her. He wanted a moment to marshal his thoughts. Normally he entered a negotiation with his plan fully worked out.

Jessica wandered into the kitchen. "Is there any wine?"

Richard motioned to the butler's pantry. "There's some Cabernet open."

"That sounds good."

She walked past him, head down. Richard watched her, looking for signs that she'd been with another man. She looked almost defeated, he thought, then rejected that idea. Jessica defeated? Never. More likely it was guilt.

She came back with the wine and took a sip. "Mmm, tastes delicious."

She looked delicious, he thought. Now that she was in the room, in the flesh, he had no difficulty remembering why he'd married her—she tantalized him. She wove a goddamned spell around him. He joked that she was a much better prescription than Viagra, but it was true. Even now, aware he was thinking of cutting her out of his life, he wanted to fill his hands with her.

"You look tired," he said.

She yawned. "I am tired. The program was so boring—mostly speeches. I could barely stay awake."

He slapped the towel against the edge of the counter. "That was a stupid lie, Jessica. So easy to check on. But it makes me wonder how many other lies you've told me."

Jessica straightened. "What are you talking about? What are you so pissed about?"

He reined in his emotions, unclenching his fists. "We had a call from Barbara Wilson about twenty minutes ago. She wanted to know if you were feeling better. That you'd called and said you were sick and couldn't attend the fundraiser."

Jessica's mouth opened, but no words came out. He'd seen that look before, usually on the face of a CEO who was trying to hide an impending bankruptcy. Richard let the silence build. He'd already said too much. The fourth Law of Power was to say less than necessary. He followed the rule now.

Jessica rallied, composing her features. "So big deal? Just because that old busybody called, you're all suspicious?"

"I just want to know why you lied to me," he said.

"No, no—it's more than that. If something is just slightly off, you immediately go to Diana and how she cheated on you." She shook back her long hair as if shaking him off.

"I've told you before, Richard, I'm not like Diana. If I wanted to have sex with someone else, I wouldn't hide the fact. I'd just tell you. So you can stop grilling me like I'm some slut."

He wanted to refute what she'd said about Diana, tell her she was full of psychobabble shit, but he held back. It would make him sound defensive, definitely not a position of strength. Instead he went on the offense.

"I'm not grilling you. I'm not saying you're like Diana. All I want from you is an answer to my question," he said. "I want to know what's going on and I want to know now."

She glared at him. "Fine, I'll tell you. I've wanted to talk to you about it anyway."

She pulled out one of the stainless steel bar stools and sat down. "I was at the doctor's."

Richard felt a moment of fear, then dismissed it. She was young and healthy. This was probably a ploy. "Are you telling me you really are sick?"

"No, I'm not telling you that. But you don't have to sound so cynical."

"Forgive me, but I've just had proof that you don't always tell the truth."

"Damn you," she said. Then she folded her hands and held them tightly together. "Okay, I'll tell you what's going on," she said without looking at him. "I took a pregnancy test last night and it was positive. I was so thrilled so I went into the doctor to check."

Richard stared at her. "What?"

"I thought I was pregnant. I was so happy." She looked at him now, her eyes filled with tears. "But it looks like I'm not."

"How the hell could you be pregnant? You're on the pill."

"No, I quit taking them a few months ago."

"You're telling me that you're trying to get pregnant?"

She nodded.

All logic fled Richard's mind. He had marshaled his strength for one battle and found himself ill prepared to deal with this one.

"Are you fucking kidding me?" he said.

She flinched at his words. "Don't swear at me! You have to understand—I want a baby. I want a baby so bad I can barely stand it."

Richard's silence this time was not planned.

"Say something," she said.

"I don't know what to say." Never in his wildest imaginings had he thought Jessica would want a baby—or that she'd go behind his back to get pregnant. "Before we got married, we agreed that there'd be no children. Remember?"

"I remember, but that was then. I'm forty now."

"That doesn't change our agreement." He felt blood throbbing in his temples. "I've got two sons and three grandchildren. I don't want any more children."

She shook her head. "I never believed that. You'd have had a vasectomy if that was true."

"What? Because I didn't have a vasectomy you thought I wanted another child? You're supposed to be on the pill. I didn't need to have a vasectomy!"

"Stop shouting at me. You don't have any feelings at all."

"No feelings? Let's talk about no feelings. I have three grandchildren you've never given a shit about. You do everything you can for us to avoid seeing them. Now, you say you want a baby? I don't get it."

"I want my own child," she said.

She reached out to touch his arm, but he leaned away.

"Richard, please. You've got to understand."

He stared at her mascara-streaked face. "I think I'm beginning to. Does this have something to do with your sister being pregnant? You two have always been so competitive."

"Of course not." She sounded indignant. "I just need to be fulfilled as a person. I realize now I need a baby to do that."

A discordant Jimi Hendrix twang sounded above her head from a speaker. Its incongruity triggered something in Richard and his mind began to clear. He saw why he'd been so conflicted. He'd begun living life on her terms, not his. That had to stop.

"You say you're not like Diana, but you've cheated on me too. Just in another way," he said.

"What are you talking about?" Jessica asked.

"You lied to me—tried to trick me."

"That's ridiculous. I just thought if I was already pregnant, you'd be happy about having a baby too."

"You really thought that? Because if you did, we are really going in completely different directions." He looked at her, his mouth set. "You need to understand, Jessica, this is not negotiable with me."

"Negotiable? We're not talking about one of your damn business deals, Richard. This is my life."

He nodded. "I get that. But we're talking about my life too. So I guess you have a big decision to make. Which is more important to you?"

"What do you mean?"

"It's fairly obvious. Which do you want more—a baby or our marriage?"

She looked stunned. "Are you talking about getting divorced?"

"I don't know. Am I?"

"Because I want a baby?"

"You wanting a baby just points out how far apart we've become," he said. He knew it was true—felt relieved that he could say it.

"God damn it, Richard. You can be such a cold bastard, you know that?"

He held back a response, just looked at her as if he felt nothing.

"I can't believe you. I tell you I want to have a child with you and you kiss me off?"

"Your screaming is not going to help the situation," Richard said, his voice cool with the detachment he was beginning to feel.

Fury distorted her features as she spun off the stool and headed out of the kitchen, her spiked heels clattering on the slate floor. When he heard the bedroom door slam, he sighed. Whatever happened, it was not going to be pretty—Jessica would make sure of that. But that he could handle. The important thing was he felt in control of his life for the first time in months.

He poured himself some of the Cabernet and went over to the refrigerator. He pulled out the lamp chops and walked outside to the patio to turn on the barbecue.

As it heated, he stood at the railing and looked out at the city. It was cold and the Space Needle, standing alone in the night sky, was barely visible. Like himself, it had gotten lost in the fog. But like himself, it would reappear.

He narrowed his eyes at the image. It was perfect.

PRIMAL FEAR

Susan hurried into the front office to check the teachers' mailboxes. She was late for work because her husband had been on the phone when she needed to leave. They'd fought about it in the car and she was still upset.

In her box was a small book of Browning's *Love Sonnets from the Portuguese*. She removed it, wondering how it had gotten there. Shrugging, she put the mystery out of her mind. She had more things to worry about than a misplaced book. She needed to concentrate on her curriculum, her students, and her home life—all in a state of flux, all in turmoil.

It was January 1968. As the civil rights movement and Vietnam protests heated up, civil and uncivil disobedience became the rule of the day. Susan's school was in Seattle's Central District—its population mainly African American. Susan was trying to update the curriculum so it would be more relevant to her students. Shakespeare wasn't cutting it.

She put the book on the table underneath the teacher boxes. Whoever had put in hers' by mistake would see it there.

She headed down the hall to her classroom. She shared it with Mr. Miller, who'd been her supervisor during her student teacher days. Maybe because of that, she still considered him an advisor.

"You've taught here for a long time," Susan had said when she met him. "I remember you from when I went here."

He looked pained by her words. "I forget sometimes how old I am."

"Things are so different now but you've stayed current. How do you reach the kids?" she'd asked.

"Being honest and being in control are good starts," he said. "You're twenty-two but you look like you're the same age as some of the students.

You're going to have to get tougher. And remember—never touch an African American kid. They see it as a sign of disrespect."

Armed with his advice, Susan began to develop her own style, one that was caring and respectfully firm. She worked on connecting with her students while learning how to maintain control of the class.

Before school or after, Mr. Miller and she were often in the classroom at the same time. Head of the English Department, he had an office adjacent to the room, so he was in and out. He was thirty-nine, stocky, with crew cut black hair and acne-pocked skin.

One afternoon, while she corrected spelling tests, he paced the room, smoking cigarette after cigarette.

"I sold my car yesterday," he said into the silence. "I traded it in for an old hearse."

"Really? A hearse?"

"Gallows humor," he said.

He began to tell her how unhappy he was at home. It wasn't the first time. His wife was a nurse on the swing shift so he rarely saw her.

"I've got nothing to do," he said. "I just sit around every night by myself and get drunk."

Susan looked up from her work. She rarely drank; sometimes at a party on weekends. She couldn't fathom someone drinking during the week. And getting drunk?

"Every night?" she asked.

He drew on his cigarette. "Yep, I like my bourbon."

Susan felt repulsed but tried not to show it. He was so nice to her. Several times he even offered to drive her home when her husband stayed late at work.

She also felt sorry for him. She had no experience with the kind of lonely alienation Mr. Miller described. She'd gone from her parents' house straight to married life. Her home was filled with love but it was no picnic. Although they'd never argued while dating, she and her husband fought all the time now. Then her father-in-law dropped dead of a heart attack on a downtown Seattle street. Her husband's grief was overwhelming him—he never got to say good-bye to the dad he idolized. He also became head of his family—which had been a mess *before* his father died. It had only gotten worse.

In the scheme of things, the book of poetry seemed unimportant. But that book remaining on the table made her uneasy. When it finally disappeared three weeks later, she felt relieved. Then she laughed at herself. Why had it even bothered her? As her husband said, she excelled at making a mountain out of a molehill.

Not long after, she received the first note. It sat on top of the book, which was again in her box.

Why did you leave the love sonnets on the table? They are for you, the note said. *They are about us.*

She looked around. Who wrote the note? Was he watching her?

She threw the note in the trash, returned the book to the table, and hurried out of the office.

When nothing happened for a week, she began to relax. Then the second note appeared in her box. It was more explicit. *Why the hell didn't you keep the book? It's yours. You're so beautiful. I want to run my hand down your leg.*

She shivered as she read the words. They scared her to her core.

Her thoughts churned that night while she fixed dinner. She just didn't get it. She was no femme fatale. She dressed like a schoolteacher in nondescript, loose-fitting dresses that came three inches below her knee. And she wasn't beautiful, not at all.

Who could it be? She thought about Dean. They drank coffee in the morning when she got there early. They had lively debates on whatever was happening in the world, usually disagreeing on each topic. It was hardly romantic.

In the next days she behaved as if she'd never seen the notes. She told no one. She was afraid to tell her husband. She'd learned that he had a hot temper, and she didn't know what he'd do. She thought about talking to Mr. Miller but decided against it. She didn't know him well enough to talk about something so embarrassing. And how would she broach the subject with her friends? Truthfully she felt sullied and ashamed. She just wanted it to all go away.

The next note arrived in her box a few days later: *I know you care for me as much as I care for you. I don't know why you are denying your feelings. We need to talk. We need to make plans. Meet me at 3:30 at the coffee shop on Galer Street.*

Her hands shaking, she looked behind her shoulder. What the hell? Whoever wrote the note was delusional. Who was it? Who was stalking her?

She almost ran from the office to her classroom. Why wouldn't this person leave her alone? Why wouldn't he stop?

She barely slept that night, waking in a daze to the clock radio alarm.

The February sky was low with gray clouds when her husband dropped her off at school. She decided to skip the office. She was afraid of what she'd find if she opened her mailbox.

In her classroom the heat hadn't come through the registers yet. She kept her coat on as she wrote lesson plans. *Concentrate*, she told herself. *Stop thinking about that note.* But the feeling of dread wouldn't lift.

The door flew open, slamming against the wall, sounding like a gunshot. She jumped and looked up.

Mr. Miller was coming fast toward her desk.

"Why didn't you meet me yesterday?" he demanded.

She gripped the edge of the desk. "I don't know what you're talking about."

"Yes, you do. I know you do because you took the note."

"How do you know about the note?"

He gave an exasperated sigh. "You know how. I wrote it."

"What?" She couldn't believe what he was saying. "No, not you."

"Of course it's me."

He loomed over the desk, the smell of alcohol on his breath. "We need to work out how to be together."

She put her hands up to stop him getting closer. "What are you talking about?"

"I love you. I want to be with you. And I know you feel the same."

He reached for her, his hand landing on her coat sleeve. She recoiled from his stubby fingers.

"Why would you think that?"

He gave her a knowing smile. "Because of all the time we spend together. And you told me to look at your legs."

"I never said that."

"Yes, you did. You said you had a run in your nylons."

Susan remembered that. She used support hose because she was on her feet all day. They were so expensive that when she snagged a pair, she'd lamented aloud about it. He thought she was suggesting he check out her legs? With support hose?

"I just said how expensive the Hanes support hose are. I didn't mean anything else."

"Now you're denying it."

"There's nothing to deny. I'm sorry you misunderstood."

He came around the desk, jerking her to her feet.

"You've been leading me on," he said.

"No, I haven't." Her voice quavered as she tried to wrench herself free. "I love my husband. I'd never think of cheating on him."

He shook her. "No, you love me!"

"Please let go of me. Please." Susan began to cry.

He dropped his hands from her arms, his anger dissipating. Instead tears filled his eyes.

"I love you," he said. "I can't live without you."

"No, that's not true," she said.

"Yes, it is." He pulled her close again, trying to kiss her. She twisted away so he couldn't get to her lips.

Then the bell rang. *Thank God*, she thought.

The door opened and a student peeked in.

"Is it all right to come in?" he asked.

"Of course, Tim. Class is about to start," Susan said.

She pulled away from Mr. Miller. He gave her a beseeching look and left the room.

She didn't see him the rest of the day. She couldn't stop shaking but somehow she'd taught her classes. She stayed in the teachers' room after school, smoking and correcting papers until her husband picked her up.

"Is everything okay?" he asked when she got into the car. "You look like you're sick."

"I'm fine," she said. "Everything's fine."

She turned the radio on to KJR. Rock and roll music flooded the car so there was no reason to talk.

Once home she went through the motions of acting normal. After dinner her husband watched a basketball game on television while she did laundry.

When she tried to fall asleep that night, she couldn't hold back her fears. She didn't want to think about what had happened, but she couldn't stop replaying the awful moments in a never-ending loop. The thought of

Mr. Miller's hands touching her made her want to vomit. What if Tim hadn't come in? What would have happened? She burrowed next to her husband, seeking his warm strength.

She felt so nauseated the next morning, she wondered if she had the flu. She thought about not going to school but forced herself to go.

Mr. Miller wasn't there. She was so relieved.

Over the weekend, keeping herself busy with the family and friends, she was fine. She didn't have to think about anything. Only at night would she succumb to the fear. In her dreams she was chased by a faceless monster.

On Monday Mr. Miller wasn't there either. During her break the principal called her into his office.

"Susan, sit down," he said.

She sat, wondering what he wanted. He'd been her ninth grade English teacher and she'd always liked him.

"You twenty-year-olds don't realize how alluring you are to a thirty-nine-year-old-man," he finally said.

"What do you mean?" she asked.

"Pat Miller tried to kill himself this weekend."

"Oh, no. How awful." Susan put a hand to her mouth.

"Yeah, he drank a bottle of bourbon and tried to slit his wrists."

"That's terrible. Is he okay?"

"His wife found him and called an ambulance. They got him to the hospital in time."

"Well, that's good," Susan managed to say.

Mr. Sheehan gave her a speculative look. "Do you care about him at all?"

Susan cringed. "Pardon me?"

"I went to see him yesterday. He told me he didn't want to live without you."

"Oh, God," she said.

"He told me he knew you felt the same."

"No! Not at all. I didn't know he was sending me those notes. I didn't know anything."

Mr. Sheehan nodded. "I thought as much."

"He's so much older. I thought of him like a father. I thought of him as a mentor. Nothing more."

"I can see that. He never had you in class. When I see you, I still think of that ninth grade kid. Which is also a mistake. You have definitely grown up into a very pretty woman."

She thought she would die right there, either of embarrassment or anguish.

"Pat is one of my best friends," he continued. "I should have seen something wasn't right. They say he's had a complete nervous breakdown."

She was horrified. Without knowing, she'd caused all of this. She couldn't hold back her tears.

Mr. Sheehan handed her a Kleenex. "You can't blame yourself. This has been brewing for a while now."

"Will he be okay?" she asked, wiping her eyes.

"I think so. They're going to hospitalize him for a couple of months." He sighed again. "Go back to your class now. I just wanted to talk to you—hear your side of things and let you know what was going on."

She stood and walked quickly from his office, not looking back.

***

Mr. Miller didn't return to school until the beginning of the following year. Susan could not look at him and stayed out of his way. He only lasted a few weeks. His nerves were so shot he couldn't teach. Even though she felt guilty, Susan was glad she didn't have to see him again.

Never up close, anyway. But for many years she often saw that hearse following her on the road. Then the fear she'd buried so deep would rise up, sending chills down her spine.

Rush To Judgment

Anne drummed her fingers on the steering wheel and wondered what was causing the traffic backup. The morning was going from bad to worse. First her ex-husband had called. By the time Ben finished his investment advice that she wouldn't accept even if it assured world peace, it was too late for her usual morning run. All she could do was take a quick shower, blow-dry her hair, and see the kids off to school.

Now 30 minutes later, she was stuck on the bridge into downtown Seattle. She'd heard the news station helicopter crisscrossing overhead several times, and listened to the traffic reports on the radio. It wasn't good.

She looked down at her running clothes. At least she could wear what she wanted to work. This way she could fit in a run during her lunch hour.

The traffic finally began to move and she put her foot down on the gas. Without warning, the cars in front of her came to an abrupt stop. Anne slammed on the brakes. Her car screeched to a halt five inches from the bumper in front of her. Before she could unwrap her white-knuckled fingers from the steering wheel, the sound of metal crunching metal filled her ears. Then her car rocked forward.

In the silence that followed, she sat completely still. Her seat belt had protected her, but she'd become an expert on whiplash injuries. She visualized herself in a neck brace. It wasn't a pretty picture.

A tapping noise startled her. She turned her head. Outside the car, a man stood, peering at her, his expression a mixture of concern and irritation. "Roll down your window," he mouthed.

"You okay?" he asked when she'd complied.

"For the moment."

The man frowned, bending to inspect her more closely. Part of Anne registered that he was seriously good looking. It was the part she didn't quite have in control. Mentally and emotionally, she'd sworn off handsome men. Physically, she sometimes still reacted. The man reached in to unlock her door. "Come on, get out. Let me see where you're hurt."

Anne looked up at him. When she was younger, his commanding tone would have thrilled her. She'd been the archetypal little maiden, waiting for her knight to rescue her. Now the arrogance that marked this Alpha male set off warning alarms in her head. She knew these kinds of men weren't dragon slayers—often they were the beasts, themselves.

She climbed out of the car. "Are you the one who hit me?"

Fists clenched at the sides of his Brooks Brothers raincoat, he nodded.

"Don't you know better than to follow too close?" she asked.

"Too close? You stopped out of nowhere!"

"Well, that's what you do when traffic ahead of you stops. Notice I didn't run into the car in front of me."

He was silent, but if looks could kill, Anne thought, she'd have a hole the size of a cannonball in her head.

"I don't mind that the law says I'm at fault," he said, a vein pulsing at his temple, "but let's be honest. You started up too fast for the flow of traffic. I bet your skid marks are under my car."

Like synchronized swimmers, Anne and he turned to look at the vehicle in question. It didn't surprise Anne that it was red, foreign, and looked expensive. He was probably some CEO in the middle of a midlife crisis like her ex-husband. She wondered if he, too, now lived with a Bambi or was it Tiffany? Anne could never remember the name of her ex-husband's girlfriend du jour.

The front of his car was as crumpled as an unmade bed. In contrast, her SUV was untouched except for a slight streak of red on its bumper.

"My car. Oh, God, my car." The man's cry of despair attracted not only Anne's attention, but that of some joggers nearby.

She watched the man pat chipped paint and twisted steel like a father soothing a wounded child. She cleared her throat. In response, he shot her a look so filled with malice, it frightened her. Was she going to come face-to-face with road rage?

"Hey, we're holding up traffic here," she said in a more reasonable tone than she'd first intended. "Why don't we call it even? You pay for your car and I'll pay for my chiropractor."

His response was not encouraging. He started towards her, looking larger and more menacing as he advanced.

"Do you know what kind of car this is?" His voice shook.

Anne backed away, ready to leap into her car if necessary. "Expensive?"

"Oh, yes. Very. But more important, a classic—an untouched classic. Never in an accident—until now."

"I'm sorry," Anne said, then wondered why. He'd hit her car. But to be fair, she had to admit he had a point. She'd started off too fast, never thinking the traffic would suddenly stop again.

"An apology? From a woman like you? Amazing."

"What do you mean, 'a woman like me'?"

"Obviously, you're one of those suburban housewives who doesn't have much to do. I don't understand why you women can't take your aerobic classes later in the day. Why not give us hard working guys a break during rush hour?"

"What do you mean, 'aerobic class'?"

He gestured at her clothing. She looked down at her "Save the Whales" tee shirt and spandex leggings, and then up at his condescending sneer. She could explain her apparel, but it wasn't relevant to the situation.

"Look, why don't we just settle this, and get on with our lives. Although you may not believe it, I have a busy schedule."

"A massage or a manicure?"

Anne stared at him. Did he actually believe what he was saying? She could barely contain her anger. She was still seething when she reached her office.

"You're late," Barbara, her assistant, said.

"I know. It's been a horrible morning. I tried to call you, but my cell phone battery was dead." Anne kicked off her running shoes. One hit the wall across the room.

"Wow, that's quite an aim. What happened? The Ex call again this morning?"

"As a matter of fact, Ben did call." Anne pulled her long, black robe over her tee shirt and leggings, and slipped on the black flats she kept under her desk.

"So that's why you're so upset."

"No, it's more than that. I had a slight accident on the bridge."

Barbara looked at her with concern. "Are you okay?"

"I'm fine, but I hate to be late."

"Oh, don't worry about that."

Anne turned away from the mirror where she'd been applying lipstick. "Why not?"

"The defense attorney for the first case this morning called to say he'd be delayed," Barbara said.

"Oh. Well, I still think I need to get out there ASAP."

She gave Barbara a smile, opened the door to the courtroom and went through. Once seated, she arranged the files in front of her. Just as she was ready to begin, the outer door to the courtroom swung open. A tall, harassed-looking man barged in.

Heaven help me, Anne thought, it's the driver of the red sports car. Had he followed her? She thought of the judge recently shot in his courtroom. Would her two children end up motherless, and living with Ben and Bimbo?

But when the man hurried to the defense table with barely a glance her way, she realized that he must be the delayed attorney. She couldn't wait for him to see her.

His look of horrified astonishment did not disappoint. And when he dropped into his seat like a duck shot during hunting season, Anne couldn't help smiling.

His worried client whispered into his ear. The lawyer nodded and stood.

"May I approach, Your Honor?" His voice was professional, if a bit grim.

"Why, of course, Counselor."

"I think in view of the circumstances, my client needs to be assigned a new judge."

She looked down at the file and found his name. "Are you saying, Mr. Metcalf, you doubt my ability to remain impartial?" She paused. "Or is it just my ability you doubt?"

"No, of course not. Neither one."

"Are you sure? Perhaps you think a woman like me could be incompetent?" She fingered her tee shirt, which was just visible at the top of her robe.

Metcalf pulled at his own collar as if it were too tight. "I apologize for this morning. I was way out of line. I guess I went a little crazy when I saw the front of my car."

Anne went for a sagacious nod. "That explains it. It was your car. That's why you began your diatribe against suburban housewives."

Metcalf closed his eyes. He's probably hoping that when he opens them, I'll have disappeared—that it will have all been a bad dream, Anne thought.

But when he did open his eyes, he also smiled. "Pretty amazing coincidence, huh?"

"Amazing." Anne had never seen him smile before, but their acquaintance had been neither long nor pleasant. It was a surprisingly nice smile.

"I said a lot of stupid things," he said.

"A lot."

"I made a complete ass out of myself."

"Complete," Anne agreed. She gestured to his client. "You need to tell him his court date will have to be changed."

Metcalf nodded. "I'll tell him."

"All right." Anne began to stand.

"Your Honor?"

She looked at Metcalf. "Yes?"

"Maybe we could go out for a coffee and discuss my stupidity further." His smile was even warmer this time.

Anne considered the idea. A coffee date? Could there be any harm in that? She'd just recently decided she had to take the plunge back into dating sometime.

She studied Defense Attorney Metcalf for a moment—the impeccable clothing, the perfect haircut, the handsome face. Was she holding all that against him? Was she stereotyping him as he had done to her? Being fair was important to Anne. Maybe, she thought, behind every pretty face didn't lurk a jerk.

Then she remembered she'd already seen him in action—how he'd treated a woman who was a stranger. She didn't need to drink coffee with him to know what was beneath his charming façade. She needed to be fair in her judgment of others, but not blind.

"No, Mr. Metcalf, I don't think that would be a wise decision," she said and brought down the gavel.

WAKING UP AT MIDNIGHT

"You son of a bitch. Get your hands off me."

The shrieking voice awakens me and I sit up dazed. In the dark, I can't see anything.

"I said get your fuckin' hands off me, you asshole."

"Shandelle, just get in the goddamn cell and shut up." This, a man's voice, slightly accented.

"You got no right to lock me in no fuckin' jail. I just be walking down the street minding my own business."

"Yeah, right. Save it for the judge."

I hear the clang of metal, then a large woman smelling of three-day-old sweat and cheap perfume looms over me. My heart pounds in my ears. I shrink back from her.

"Who the hell are you?" she demands.

More to the point, who is she and what's she doing in my dream? Because I have to be dreaming. What would I be doing in a jail cell? I've never even gotten a speeding ticket.

My dreams have been weird for months. When Mac died, I couldn't sleep at all. His place in our bed was too cold—it froze the sleep right out of me. Now I take sleeping pills. Maybe that's why my dreams seem so real I feel I'm awake. I dream often about the homeless woman, the one with eyes like a vacant lot, who sits in front of the grocery store.

"Hey, I asked you a question. Who are you? What the hell are you doing here?"

I shut my eyes, praying that when I open them, I'll see the familiar outline of my bedroom window. But that doesn't happen. And instead of the soft fabric of my headboard behind me, I feel the cold hardness of cement. Besides, Shandelle's grip on my arm is too painful to be an illusion.

"My name is Joanna MacDonald." I have to pause for a moment to let the panic settle a bit. "I don't know where I am, let alone why I'm here."

Shandelle snorts and pulls me up by my coat sleeves. She drags me towards the front of the cell where a dim light slots through the bars. What is she going to do to me? My whole body begins to shake.

"Jesus Fuckin' Christ. Ain't you a sorry sight."

"What do you mean?"

"Girl, you got an eye that's comin' up black, blue and purple, and there's cuts all over your damn cheeks. And look at your coat. You got blood all over it, too."

I look down my front. Shandelle's not exaggerating. Dried blood is spattered over my coat like it's a Jackson Pollock canvas. "My God."

"What happen? Your ol' man beat you up?"

"My husband's dead."

"You kill him? That why you here? Must be, 'cuz if he beat you up, he'd be in jail 'stead of you." Her face glows with prurient curiosity.

"My husband died of cancer six months ago."

"Oh, cancer. That all?"

That was enough for Mac, and for me, I want to say, but Shandelle's squinting up close to me, crowding me further. I lean back until the bars of the cell stop me. The coldness of their steel shafts burns my shoulders even as they support me.

"So tell me," Shandelle says, "why you're here."

"I really don't know. The last thing I remember is turning off the light to go to sleep. I think it was about ten o'clock."

"Well, it's 'bout three in the morning, now. You lost yourself five hours somewhere."

"Five hours?" I can't help shivering. I reach out a hand to Shandelle. "You have to help me. I just don't know what's going on."

Shandelle pushes me away. "You crazy or something?"

"I don't think so."

"On drugs, then?"

"No, of course not." Joanna MacDonald on drugs? I almost laugh at the idea. "I just take some medications the doctor gave me."

Shandelle's smile is mocking. "Just some medications. Right. I'm guessing they ain't no over the counter shit."

"No, they're prescription. I was pretty nervous around Christmas. It was our first without Mac—you know, my husband. I had a panic attack in the grocery store."

I use my thumb to wipe away saliva in the corner of my mouth. "I thought I was having a heart attack so I drove to the doctor. He said it was just a panic attack. He gave me some tranquilizers, and some sleeping pills so I could sleep."

"How about the alcohol you drinking? I can smell it on your breath."

"For God's sake, I had a glass or two of wine tonight." My fear is diminishing at an inverse ratio to my annoyance.

"Sure you did. A blackout comes on from one glass of wine? Tell me another one."

"A blackout? What are you talking about?"

"Didn't you say you can't remember nothin' after going to bed?"

"That's right."

"And now you're here and you don't know how you got here. Ain't that right?"

I nod.

"Well, let me tell you something. You don't wake up in no jail cell, in the middle of the night, not remembering nothing, without being on something."

With that pronouncement, Shandelle turns and sashays to the back of the tiny cell. I can't tell if her walk is influenced by her stiletto heels and tight skirt, or the alcohol I definitely smell on her breath.

"This place is a shit hole," she grumbles, settling onto the bench where I'd been lying down.

Left alone by the cell door, I feel exposed by the light. Questions tumble through my brain. Shandelle has to be right. I must have had a blackout, and I had to have broken a law. But what had I done? My head throbs as I push myself to remember. But it's useless. I give up and go to sit on the remaining bench in the cell.

Lost in thought, I finger my coat collar, encountering a crustiness congealed on the wool. I peer down and see the tell-tale rust of dried blood.

"Oh, God!" I pull off the coat, almost ripping it my haste. Underneath, I find I'm wearing my flannel nightgown. I'd left my house dressed like this? At night, in the middle of winter? I look down at my feet. At least I'm wearing boots.

"Mother fuck. It's going to be a long enough night as it is without you shouting and mumbling every fucking minute. Shut up and go to sleep," Shandelle snaps.

Kicking the coat away from me, I lie down. The cold metal makes me shiver, but I'm afraid to use the blanket at the end of the bench. How many other people must have used it? I already feel so grimy, especially my hands and under my nails. Is this how the homeless woman in front of the market feels? As if she were basted in dirt?

I touch my cheek. I feel a cut that goes all the way down to my chin. "Oh, God." I whisper it this time.

It's not a prayer. I gave up on God when Mac got sick. I'd always believed that everything would turn out for the best if you just worked hard enough to make it happen. I found out what a lie that was while I watched Mac die inch-by-inch. It hadn't mattered what I did or how hard I prayed— nothing stopped the cancer from taking over his body.

I had tried to be so strong for him and for the kids. "You were a rock through it all," Dr. Madigan said when he wrote me the prescription for Valium.

If I'd been a rock for all of them, Mac, Kimberly and Eric, I've now crumbled into dust. Every day feels as if I am wading through JELL-O—I can't get the smallest task done. Like my New Year's resolution to clean out Mac's clothes and give them away. Kimberly had told me it was time. So I'd gone in the closet, but came away only with one of Mac's sweatshirts. It still smells like him. I sleep with it.

Shandelle's snore startles me. I close my eyes, trying to stay calm. I'm afraid I'll cry, and that is one thing I've sworn not to do. When Mac had been diagnosed with pancreatic cancer two years ago, he'd begged me not to cry—it hurt him too much, he said. So I'd promised him I wouldn't cry anymore. And I hadn't. Not through the months of chemo. Not when he became so thin, I could see the bones sticking out on his frame. Not when he died. Not at the funeral.

"Now is not the time to break my promise," I whisper into the stale air, but it's too late. I shouldn't have closed my eyes so tight. It's facilitated the tears instead of holding them back. They fall down my cheeks with a life of their own.

"I'm sorry, Mac. So sorry I failed you."

I wrap my arms around my middle, and rock back and forth.

How soon I fall asleep I don't know, but my new dream is as vivid as my reality. Kim, Eric and I are in Volunteer Park having a picnic. I'm scooping potato salad onto paper plates when I look up and see Mac watching us.

"Mac," I call out, overjoyed to see him. He turns away as if he hadn't heard me, and begins to climb up a grassy knoll. I call his name again, but he won't stop, won't even turn around. He just keeps walking away from me towards a beam of light.

The light becomes blinding. I struggle to keep my eyes wide open so I can follow Mac, but it's impossible.

"Hey, lady, open your eyes again. I want to talk to you! Don't pretend you're asleep."

The voice grates at me, loud and insistent. I'm not sure where it comes from. My dream? Where am I?

It's Shandelle's "Shut the fuck up" that reminds me. I sit up, already shaking. Light from something beyond the cell targets my face.

"You shut the fuck up, Shandelle," the voice says. "And you, lady, yeah, you, come over here."

His menacing tone propels me off the bench and towards the bars. I shield my eyes from the bright glare.

A key turns in the lock and I take heart. They've realized their mistake, and they're going to let me go.

"Come out of there and put your hands behind your back," the man orders.

"What?"

"I said, put your hands behind your back. You fuckin' deaf or something?"

I do as he says. There's a clicking sound and I find myself handcuffed.

"Okay, come with me." He gives me a shove, then turns and locks the cell door.

"Up the stairs," he orders.

I stumble ahead of him, disoriented, not knowing where I'm going— him so close I can feel his breath on the back of my neck. Who is he? What's going to happen now? Visions of police brutality whirl in my head and I long for the relative comfort of Shandelle.

By the time we reach the top of the stairs, I'm gulping for air.

"Hold it." The man reaches around me to unlock the door. He pushes it open and me through it. I stumble again, blinded by the sudden fluorescent lighting.

The man's harsh voice rasps in my ear, "Still drunk, huh?"

He grabs my arm and pulls me along a corridor that has offices on either side. I hear a radio blaring music from one of them.

I turn my head so I can see my tormentor. He looks like a street person. His clothes are as dirty and torn as he is. Red scratch marks, oozing tiny dots of blood, punctuate the stubble of his swarthy cheeks.

We pass a uniformed police officer, the Seattle Police Department badge prominent on his chest. I throw him a pleading look, but he ignores me, just as Mac had done in my dream.

"Hey, Ed. Got another homeless weirdo?" The officer gestures towards me. "She do that to your face? Looks like you had a fight with your razor and lost."

Ed. Now I know his name, at least.

"Fuck you," Ed tells the officer, and tightens his grip on my arm.

"Ouch." I jerk away instinctively.

Ed raises his fist close to my face. "I'm telling you, lady, don't give me any more trouble."

"I'm not giving you any trouble. You squeezed my arm and it hurt."

The uniformed officer steps forward, a grin on his face. "You need any assistance?"

"Go to hell," Ed says, and grabs me again.

Halfway down the hall, he pushes me into a room. Little more than a cubicle, it's furnished with a metal table and chairs.

"Sit down." Ed shuts the door behind him.

I try to follow this direction, but I have trouble finding the seat of the chair without the use of my hands.

He sits in front of me, his legs straddling the chair backwards.

I stare at him, glad to be able to see him fully. He's wearing a plaid flannel jacket over a faded blue T-shirt, ripped jeans and tennis shoes with holes in them. His nose is hawkish, and the planes of his face, sharp—the scratches marking it like a road map. Dark eyes, etched with lines, watch me as I look at him.

"Who are you?" My throat is so dry that the question comes out as a croak.

"Cut the crap," he says.

"What do you mean?"

"Listen, lady, you and I already went a couple of rounds tonight, and my patience is shot to shit."

"What do you mean?"

He swears again and stands, knocking his chair against one of the walls. "What's your name?" he yells.

I flinch back from him. "Joanna MacDonald."

"Speak up."

"Joanna MacDonald," I say louder.

"Well, well, an answer, finally." He backs off, and pulls a cigarette out of a pack in his shirt pocket. "Okay, Joanna MacDonald. Where do you live?"

"I live on Federal Avenue, and I'll tell you anything you want to know."

"Oh, really? Like what were you doing walking around Broadway with only a nightgown and an overcoat on in the middle of the night?"

"What? I was doing what?"

"You're doing it again, lady. Acting like you never were out of your mind drunk and you didn't scratch the fuck out of my face. Where do you think you got that blood all over you? You want a fucking DNA test to prove it's mine?"

"No." I look away. "No."

The room is so small that if I hadn't been handcuffed, I could reach out and touch the walls on either side. As they start to close in on me, my heart pounds in my ears.

"I don't feel well," I manage to say.

The man—Ed—looks up from lighting his cigarette. "That's what booze will do to you."

"No, no, you're wrong. There's some mistake. I've never been drunk in my life. I'd never do that."

I almost tell him about my father. That mean old World War II vet drank every night and made it hell for all of us. I'd vowed never to be like that. "And I didn't have too much to drink tonight. I had a glass of wine with my dinner, and a glass while I watched television."

He looks at me as if he doesn't believe a word.

"But even if I had too much to drink and I passed out, why would I leave my house?" I ask.

"Who knows?" He swings onto the chair, backwards again, and exhales a stream of smoke. "What else you using?"

"Using?"

"Yeah, you taking any drugs?"

"Do you mean like heroin?"

"You being a smart ass with me? I wouldn't if I were you." Ed scowls at me while he pulls out a notebook and a pen from a pocket. "What's the names of what you're taking?"

"The doctor prescribed sleeping pills so I could sleep, and tranquilizers so I could relax. My husband just died and I haven't been able to do either—sleep or relax, that is."

Ed shakes his head, muttering something under his breath, as he writes in the notebook.

I stare at the lines of red stretching down his cheeks. "I really did that to you?"

"I got no reason to lie."

"I just can't believe it." My stomach roils at the thought of what I'd done during my blackout. "I'm afraid I'm going to be sick."

"Shit." He tips his chair backward to reach a wastebasket in the corner behind him.

"Here, use this." He shoves it against my leg.

"Please, can't I use the restroom?"

"No way. Not until I get some more answers."

I lean over my knees, breathing in through my nose and exhaling through my mouth. The handcuffs restrict my movement—my shoulders feel like they're coming out of their sockets. Shandelle was right about you, I think. You are an asshole, and I'll be damned if I'll give you the satisfaction of throwing up in front of you.

I gulp down the nausea and take two more deep breaths.

"You didn't lose your dinner, after all," he says when I sit up.

This last piece of sarcasm takes the rest of my fear and spins it into anger. "Go to hell," I say with a shaking defiance. I'd thought of using the F-word that was so popular here, but I couldn't quite get my mouth around the word.

He stubs out his cigarette with short, jerky movements. "What the hell are you smiling for? You're in a fucking lot of trouble."

"That isn't exactly a news flash." I'm proud of how sarcastic I sound. I start to laugh.

He bangs his fist on the table. "Stop laughing, God dammit."

I jump, and then start laughing harder. I can't help it.

He grabs my upper arm. "Stop it!"

He doesn't let go of me until I get my laughter under control.

"Who are you?" It's not the same question he asked before. His tone is different—puzzled sounding.

"I told you. I'm Joanna MacDonald. Although, I'm not sure who that is, now. I used to be Mac's wife. I used to be a school librarian. But I'm neither of these things anymore."

"School librarian?"

"Uh huh, in a middle school. I loved it, but I had to quit when, Mac—my husband—got so sick." I look up from my study of the floor. "And I'm here and you've put me in handcuffs. And you say I scratched your face like that."

"You don't remember me coming up to you on the street and asking you if you needed any help?" His voice is less harsh than before.

"No, I've been trying to remember. I remember eating my sandwich and then going into the den. I remember going upstairs to bed. I even remember brushing my teeth and turning out the light, but then I woke up in that cell. I haven't a clue to what happened in between."

He sits smoking and staring at me for what seems a long time. I look back at him, almost without blinking. Then, something inside me shifts. I'm aware that the movement to create this change has been progressing for the last hour, as if I've been on an elevator that has been in descent and now has settled on the bottom floor. I've gone from abject fear to an inner calmness.

"I've been as honest with you as I can," I say, breaking the silence. "I don't think you can keep me in here without charging me or letting me make at least one phone call." I am about to say I want to call my daughter, but then I think better of it. Kimberly will be humiliated by what has happened. If Eric were in town, I could call him. But he is back at college.

"You already got your chance. You don't remember?"

I shake my head. "Who did I call?"

"I don't know, but there wasn't any answer."

I'm quiet for a moment, wondering what number I'd called. It's all so strange—to have done so many things without any memory of it. I feel the nausea begin to rise again, and force myself to back away from those thoughts.

"Don't you have to read me my rights or something?" I ask.

He looks at me with exasperation. "I already did."

"Oh, well, I guess I don't remember that, either." Again I look down at the peeling floor and then back up at him. "But even so, I'm not answering any more questions."

"Fine. I'll just take you back to detention, then. Stand up and turn around."

I do as his says and he unlocks the handcuffs. It feels like heaven to be able to move my arms.

"Thanks," I say.

He grunts something in reply, but I'm not fooled. His action shows a kindness he wants to mask. And, of course, that he no longer thinks I am a risk. Such a small thing, but it lifts a weight off my heart.

The return trip downstairs is uneventful. Shandelle is still snoring when Ed locks me back into the cell. He walks away without another word.

"Officer?" I call to him. "Ed."

He wheels around and comes back to the cell door. "My name is Eduardo, not Ed. Eduardo Martinez."

"Sorry. I just heard the other officer call you Ed."

"Well, that guy's a fuck head."

"I'm sure he is." I pause, waiting for the sneer on his face to subside. "Officer Martinez?"

"Yeah?"

"I just wanted to say I'm sorry about your face. I must not have realized you were a police officer." I gesture to his rumpled clothing. "I must have thought I was being attacked. It's the only thing that makes sense to me."

He shrugs. "Yeah. Yeah. Like I always say, 'Save it for the judge.'"

When he's gone, I walk to my makeshift bed and sit down. It's strange, but I feel almost happy. I'd thought I wanted to die when Mac had. Only my children had kept me from giving up totally. But tonight I'd feared for my life several times. With each threat, I relearned how precious life is. What will happen in the morning? I don't know that.

Shandelle stirs, muttering something in her sleep.

In the slate steel twilight of the cell, I sigh. Then I lie down and pull the coarse wool blanket around me.